MAGESTORM

Kozma Himmlisch stabbed his fingers towards Gerhart. Blinding bolts of light burst from their tips, zigzagging their way through the downpour. Several bolts struck the rooftop in front of him, exploding tiles and blasting shards of stone from the tower. The rest of the miniature lightning strikes slammed into Gerhart's body, hurling him backwards.

His mind-flame guttered in the darkness, but did not go out.

'Your move, I believe,' Kozma sneered over the drumming of the rain.

A WARHAMMER NOVEL

MAGESTORM

JONATHAN GREEN

For Clare, for everything

A BLACK LIBRARY PUBLICATION

First published in Great Britain in 2004 by
BL Publishing,
Games Workshop Ltd.,
Willow Road, Nottingham,
NG7 2WS, UK

10 9 8 7 6 5 4 3 2 1

Cover illustration by Adrian Smith,
Map by Nuala Kennedy.

A CIP record for this book is available from the British Library

ISBN 1 84416 074 2

Distributed in the US by Simon & Schuster
1230 Avenue of the Americas, New York, NY 10020, US.

Printed and bound in Great Britain by
Cox & Wyman Ltd, Reading, Berkshire, UK

See the Black Library on the Internet at
www.blacklibrary.com

Find out more about Games Workshop
and the world of Warhammer at
www.games-workshop.com

THIS IS A DARK age, a bloody age, an age of daemons and of sorcery. It is an age of battle and death, and of the world's ending. Amidst all of the fire, flame and fury it is a time, too, of mighty heroes, of bold deeds and great courage.

AT THE HEART of the Old World sprawls the Empire, the largest and most powerful of the human realms. Known for its engineers, sorcerers, traders and soldiers, it is a land of great mountains, mighty rivers, dark forests and vast cities. And from his throne in Altdorf reigns the Emperor Karl-Franz, sacred descendent of the founder of these lands, Sigmar, and wielder of his magical warhammer.

BUT THESE ARE far from civilised times. Across the length and breadth of the Old World, from the knightly palaces of Bretonnia to ice-bound Kislev in the far north, come rumblings of war. In the towering World's Edge Mountains, the orc tribes are gathering for another assault. Bandits and renegades harry the wild southern lands of the Border Princes. There are rumours of rat-things, the skaven, emerging from the sewers and swamps across the land. And from the northern wildernesses there is the ever-present threat of Chaos, of daemons and beastmen corrupted by the foul powers of the Dark Gods. As the time of battle draws ever near, the Empire needs heroes like never before.

ONE
The Tower of Heaven

*'And the name of the Fourth Lore of Magic is the
Wind of Azyr. It is by means of the magical energies of Azyr that the Astromancer may discern
events yet to come in the movement of the Celestial Bodies as they wend their way across the
Heavens. Hence the Fourth Lore of Magic is also
known as the Lore of the Heavens.'*

– Taken from the *Liber Artes Magicae*

THUNDER BROKE ACROSS the tortured heavens loud; it
seemed to shatter the sky. It was as if the hammer of
Lord Sigmar had smote the firmament and, at its
thunderous impact, the storm broke. Rain fell down
from the grey-black clouds in a torrential downpour.
Lightning sparked throughout the roiling thunderheads that covered the dome of the sky from one

horizon to the next: from north to south, east to west. Even though it was only mid-afternoon on a spring day in Jahrdrung, the cloud cover was so dense that it was almost as dark as night.

Rain lashed the scrubby moors of this wild wilderness that lay in the shadow of the Middle Mountains, with Hergig a clear six leagues to the south. Gale-force winds drove fat greasy raindrops through the thick canopy of darkly brooding forest, and tore leaves from their branches. The deluge pounded the ground, turning turf to a sodden bog and churning the tracks that passed for roads in these parts into a sucking quagmire. Runnels formed all over the uplands, newly birthed streams brought forth by the cloudburst, and went coursing down the hillsides. These fed rain-swollen streams that in turn fed rushing tributaries. They all converged to become a raging torrent of white water that plunged over the jagged boulders of rapids through the gorge at the foot of a rugged, storm-scarred hilltop – the highest piece of land for several leagues around.

Stark against the horizon, at the summit of the craggy hill, a lone black tower pierced the storm-wracked sky like an accusing finger pointing at the heavens – furious that the storm should obscure the heavens from the gaze of the observatory at its summit.

The storm crashed around the tower, as if it were the focus for the tempest's wrath. Lightning split the sky again, bathing the hilltop in a momentary dazzling light. The lightning glittered from each leaded pane of the tower's glass dome.

Rain drummed down on the roof of the observatory and the flat roof of the tower next to it. It had been raining heavily for the last five days and there was no sign of it abating.

There was another vivid flash of light only this time it came from the top of the tower itself, blazing out from inside the glittering dome. It turned the observatory into a beacon of light in the middle of the grey-black wilderness.

With a crash of splintering glass, part of the star gazing dome exploded outwards as a figure smashed through it and slid to a halt on the wet stones of the tower's flat roof. Rain pelted down, heavy as a monsoon, soaking the figure's scorched and ruddy robes before the straggly-haired man could raise himself groggily.

'Curses!' the man muttered. Gerhart Brennend hated the rain.

Looking back towards the glass dome he could see the figure of his rival clearly framed in the shattered broken panes. In front of it splinters of glass shone on the rooftop like a thousand sparkling diamonds.

Gerhart made a hasty assessment of his situation. His sword-belt was still securely fastened about his waist, and his sword was in its scabbard at his side. His staff had landed close by. Taking hold of the gnarled and knotted rod of oak he got to his feet and prepared to face the force of the celestial wizard's wrath. The astromancer, Kozma Himmlisch, was striding out into the gale to face him.

Years of experience fighting upon battlefields across the length and breadth of the Empire helped him focus, despite the distracting rain that drove into his face and the injuries he had already suffered. The storm winds howled around him but now he could feel other winds blowing their own course about him. Many followed the howling path of the gale but some flowed contrary to the rest, whirling in eddies and battling against the vortices of the storm.

Despite the steady, striding approach of his opponent, Gerhart closed his eyes.

He pictured a black void in his mind, and there – in the heart of the darkness – a flame flickered into life. The yellow and orange tongue of flame, white-hot at its core, writhed and grew. Gerhart could feel its warmth in the palms of his hands where he clutched the staff. He opened his eyes again and, glancing down at the backs of his hands saw that the hairs were beginning to dry out.

Kozma Himmlisch halted. Gerhart stood hunched, ready to defend himself, favouring his right leg, his left knee having been smashed as he hurtled through the dome of the observatory. The celestial wizard stood tall, his stance suggesting an unwavering arrogant trust in his own abilities.

Where Gerhart's robes were a deep red, his rival's rich blue garments, picked out with gold embroidered stars and silver-threaded crescent moons, seemed to shimmer and glisten in the rain, making them appear more regal and luxurious.

Where Gerhart appeared bedraggled and unkempt, his long greying black hair matted against the side of his face, Kozma seemed invigorated by the energy of the storm, as if he had drawn power from it. His white curled beard was immaculately trimmed, not a hair was out of place. Gerhart's almost white drooping moustaches and the point of his beard sagged under the weight of water.

The celestial wizard's crown-like sorcerer's hat, also blue and trimmed with gold, was emblazoned with a crest of the comet of power at the front. It sat securely on the wizard's head, despite the clash that had just taken place in the observatory. Gerhart's own pate was bald, except for one last stubborn tuft of black hair. The rain was making it glisten. Water ran into his thickly curling eyebrows and from there into his eyes.

The astromancer took a step forward and glared at Gerhart, his gaze as piercing as the stars glittering against the cloth of night. Gerhart met his opponent's stare and raised his staff, holding it defensively across his body.

'Enough of these games,' the celestial wizard said, his voice clear and sharp as it carried to Gerhart over the wailing of the wind and the ominous rumbles of thunder. 'Now we battle to the death.'

'That is your choice,' Gerhart growled, the flickering flame in his mind growing in size and intensity.

'Or should I say, your death?' Kozma went on, as if he hadn't heard his opponent.

Quick as lightning, Kozma Himmlisch stabbed his fingers towards Gerhart. Blinding bolts of light burst from their tips, zigzagging their way through the downpour. Several bolts struck the rooftop in front of him, exploding tiles and blasting shards of stone from the tower. The rest of the miniature lightning strikes slammed into Gerhart's body, hurling him backwards.

His mind-flame guttered in the darkness, but did not go out.

'Your move, I believe,' Kozma sneered over the drumming of the rain.

Steam rose from his soaking robes where he had been struck by the sorcerer's spell. Gerhart rolled onto his side and got to his feet once more. He ached all over. He had suffered some small cuts when he had gone through the dome, and they stung in the rain. His right knee flared with pain every time he put weight on it. His left shoulder felt as if it might be broken, at best badly bruised.

Every point on his body felt like it had been hit with a blacksmith's hammer. The pain did not trouble him unduly. He had suffered worse in his years as a battle wizard among the armies of the Empire, before his untimely exile from the Bright order. And besides, another emotion was helping him to suppress the pain of the injuries: he could feel himself beginning to lose his temper. And Gerhart Brennend's temper was a dangerous thing indeed.

'Kozma, you go too far,' he told the celestial sorcerer through gritted teeth. He began to swing his staff around his head. 'I warn you, do not provoke me.'

As the blackened oak staff described a circle through the rainy air above him, Gerhart focussed on the flame flickering in his mind, feeding it with the fuel of his rising fury. A spark fizzed and died at the swinging end of the staff.

Kozma had been watching Gerhart's efforts with an expression of mild amusement. At this he let out a laugh.

'What's the matter, old friend?' he sneered. 'Is the rain affecting your ability to spell-weave?'

Barely suppressed rage bubbled beneath the grim set of Gerhart's gaunt features. He glared at Kozma and swung the staff harder and faster.

With an audible *whoosh* the end of the staff burst into flame. Gerhart kept the oak rod moving and instead of the wind and rain putting the flame out, the staff began to leave a trail of fire in its wake. The atmosphere around the top of the tower was, after all, saturated in magical power. It was merely a case of isolating the current he required and drawing it into himself. His natural propensity for manipulating fire could do the rest.

Gerhart could feel the wind of Aqshy blowing gently against his face, warm as a homecoming hearth on his cheeks. It was drying the strands of hair at his temples. Admittedly, the flaming trail left by the burning end of the staff was not as great as he had hoped, but to conjure such a flame in the middle of a thunderstorm required great expertise.

With one last great effort, Gerhart swung the blazing end of the staff towards the celestial wizard, extending his reach in only one hand. A stream of orange fire roared from the red-coal tip, eating up the oxygen in the air between the two sorcerers and casting its orange glow over the top of the tower. The fiery blast hit the rain-slicked robes of the celestial wizard and obscured Kozma Himmlisch from Gerhart's view momentarily.

The fire in his mind's eye blazed brightly for a few seconds and then subsided to a flickering candle flame once more. With a wet hiss the rain doused the burning brand of the fire wizard's staff. The orange reflections from the rain-slicked roof vanished to be replaced by the night-like gloom of the glowering storm, punctuated by bursts of acid white light along the horizon. The warm wind blowing on Gerhart's face cooled too, until only the chill of the damp air remained.

Gerhart looked up at the celestial wizard, uncertain of what to expect. What little hope he might have had for his opponent's demise faded as he saw Kozma Himmlisch smiling back at him, seemingly untouched. Gerhart's spell had had no effect; how could he have been so foolish to expect otherwise in such weather? His powers as a fire mage were severely weakened thanks to the rain.

Gerhart's anger at his own naive thoughts fed the flames of his fury. But before he could put it to good use there was another retina-searing explosion of light and Gerhart flew backwards once more. The blast was the strongest the celestial wizard had produced yet. Gerhart's arms were flung outwards from his body in an involuntary spasm, as the massive surge of electrical energy coursed through his body. His staff flew from his hand.

Some small part of Gerhart that was still aware of what was going on told him that this was it. Kozma's attacks had steadily pushed him back towards the edge of the tower's battlements. This last almighty blast would surely send him over the edge and down to his death on the rugged crag top one hundred feet below.

There was the sound of cracking mortar and Gerhart came to an abrupt halt as he slammed into something cold and hard.

In his mind's eye the flame was slowly extinguished.

Weakened by Kozma's relentless attacks the fire wizard almost blacked out. Pain that even his furious temper could not quash stabbed through his spine. His head sagged onto his chest, as he lay stricken at the edge of the roof, his back resting awkwardly on something behind him.

Gerhart looked up, his head lolling back on his neck. Blinking the rain from his eyes he tried to focus on what it was that had stopped his death-plunge so abruptly. He saw a tall copper rod protruding from the side of the tower, glinting in the flickering epileptic light of the tempest. A lightning conductor, its tip fashioned in the form of an arrow-point.

The metal pole swayed violently in the wind. Gerhart's collision with the lightning rod had almost smashed it completely free of its mounting. Next to it a battered weather vane spun crazily in the tornado winds.

'You would come here,' Kozma was saying, the pitch of his voice rising, 'to my tower, to my home, and attempt to kill me? Then you are an idiot as well as a traitor! Where would I be better able to protect myself than here, surrounded by the very source of my power?'

Shaking his head to help bring him to his senses, Gerhart turned back to the astromancer. The sorcerer was advancing towards him across the rooftop, the sparkling dome of the observatory behind him. Raw blue-white energy crackled from his fingertips and sparked from the coal-black orbs of his eyes. The glass shards scattered across the flat roof reflected the lightning like a myriad of tiny mirrors, dazzling Gerhart.

Gerhart could see the sorcerous winds swirling around him in a dancing vortex of power, like ribbons of some multi-hued substance. He glimpsed images within the whirling eddies and pulled on the currents, like faces briefly captured in thunderclouds or esoteric runes of mystical power.

'Now you will pay for your insolence!' Kozma spat. 'It is time to die, old friend.'

This was it, Gerhart realised. The celestial wizard's next attack would surely mean the end for the fire mage unless he did something quickly. It was now or never.

Aware of a low chanting coming from Kozma, Gerhart hauled himself to his feet, using the metal shaft of the lightning conductor for support. He prayed desperately to whatever deity might be listening that, in spite of the storm raging around him, that an unexpected lightning strike would not strike the conductor while he was clinging to it. The metal pole rocked unsteadily as the suffering wizard put all his weight against it.

Through the dark rain, Gerhart could see that the pole rising above the top of the tower was merely the tip of the lightning conductor, a patina of verdigris covering its surface. The rest of the metal shaft was attached to the outside of the tower and descended all the way to the ground, where it would earth all lightning strikes. An iron staple hammered into the stone of the roof connected the two parts. The arrow-point tip of the lightning rod had also been mortared into place at the top of the crenellated battlements.

Only half aware now of the dull chanting voice of the celestial wizard, and drawing on the last reserves of his strength, Gerhart hugged the lightning conductor and then let his tired body sag. With a tortured rending of metal, the rod bent over at its base. Gerhart could feel the hairs on the back of his neck begin to rise as a massive static charge built around him. Kozma Himmlisch was obviously determined that the fire wizard wasn't going to walk away from this final, fatal blast.

Gerhart gave the broken mortar around the base of the pole a vicious kick, the heel of his leather boot pounding the ancient lime to powder. He gave the lightning conductor another sharp tug, sending renewed daggers of pain stabbing through his spine, and the tip came away from the battlements in his hands.

With his hair now standing out from the sides of his head, Gerhart turned to face the astromancer. Kozma was charged with the power of the heavens, his hair too standing on end. The sorcerer yelled the last words of his incantation over the wailing roar of the storm and drew his arms back, ready to fling his spell with full force.

The lightning conductor gripped firmly in his right hand, Gerhart brought his arm back before hurling it forwards again sharply. Just then Kozma unleashed the full fury of the tempest at him. Pain tore through his shoulder but Gerhart's aim was true.

The metal shaft twisted through the air, glittering in the light of the energy streaking from the celestial sorcerer's hands. A jagged bolt of forked lightning streaked down from the tormented sky above.

The spear-tip point of the lightning conductor pierced the wizard's chest below the sternum and burst from his back in a gout of black blood. An eye-bulging expression of horror briefly appeared on Kozma's face before the full force of the storm was drawn inexorably to the lightning rod.

Kozma Himmlisch was destroyed in a blaze of blinding white light. It bathed the entire tower in its cold, burning brightness. It also blazed the image of the celestial wizard being burnt to a crisp onto the back of Gerhart's eyes so that it was all he could see until the glaring light faded back to normal.

Lightning continued to course down from the broiling clouds above, channelled by the lightning conductor. Kozma's spell was now horribly out of control. One whole side of the tower was exploded by the blast. With a boom that Gerhart felt through his feet, masonry tumbled from the battlements and crashed onto the sodden ground below. The wind and rain swept into exposed chambers within the tower like hungry animals. They ravaged the shelves of books and scrolls in the astromancer's library in their fury, sending sheaves of papers flapping out in a savage squall.

Gerhart surveyed the devastation as he teetered on the brink of a crumbling precipice. His body was shaking, pain seeming to split his body apart from the inside out and the outside in. He had not been left unscathed by the devastation around him. Blood ran from his face and hands where splinters of stone had struck his exposed skin.

As well as the structural damage suffered by the tower, the observatory had caught fire, though this was the result of the lightning rather than any spell cast by the fire wizard. The fire raged in spite of the harsh ferocity of the storm. The rain now whipping in through the shattered glass dome had yet to douse the ravenous flames.

Kozma's body lay a few feet from Gerhart, an unrecognisable fire-consumed carcass, the twisted and melted spear of the lightning rod still transfixing it.

The fire wizard stumbled forwards as the roof of the tower shifted beneath him. He picked up his fallen staff and hurried into the relative safety of the burning observatory. He heard a number of stone skitter down the side of the tower as they came free from where he had been standing moments before.

Flames were licking around the shattered crystal dome of the astromancer's lair, the lightning strikes having set light to the rugs and the dry dusty tomes cluttering the bookshelves against the stone wall of the chamber. This wall was Gerhart's means of escape. An unassuming archway in the middle led to the spiral stone staircase that descended the levels of the tower to the ground.

Hot air swept around him, carrying glowing orange embers out into the still raging storm. The bright wizard drew some comfort from the presence of the conflagration but he still felt drained after the expulsion of so much magical energy. And his body was wracked with pain.

But for one educated at the renowned colleges of magic in Altdorf, the destruction of the observatory cut Gerhart to the core. To see such precious and rare books and scrolls, which had been collected by Kozma Himmlisch over many decades, being consumed by the flames, not to mention the knowledge they contained, did nothing but fuel Gerhart's own abating anger.

A huge baroque telescope dominated the observatory. An amalgamation of lenses, mirrors, calibrated measures and gleaming polished tubes, the telescope was as big as the legendary steam tanks of the Imperial gunnery schools, and its main scope looked even more impressive than the cannon-muzzles of the incredible war engines.

The whole contraption had been carefully counterweighted so that it could be manoeuvred on a series of cog-toothed rails. Caught in the heart of the blaze consuming the observatory dome, the delicate labour of skilled engineers and artisans was being lost to the fire. Delicate brass scopes melted and warped amidst the flames and finely ground lenses cracked under the intense heat.

There was not much Gerhart could do for the telescope. But there were other, greater prizes awaiting him amidst the papers covering the large desk that dominated the chamber. Staggering over to it, Gerhart began to rummage through the open books and unrolled scrolls littering its surface, as yet barely touched by the flames. Amidst the volumes concerning the movements of celestial bodies and star charts there were scraps of parchment that bore the scrawl of a hasty, desperate hand. They contained peculiar diagrams and images that appeared to be those of a twin-tailed shooting star, as well as hurriedly drawn maps of the Old World with sweeping arrows descending from the north.

As he searched, sparks whirled around him from the swelling, hungry fire, threatening to ignite the flammable materials covering the desk. Gerhart slapped at the embers as they tumbled towards the precious papers, quenching them with the sodden sleeves of his rain-soaked robes. The ink on the pieces of parchment began to run but the fire wizard did not seem to care.

A hasty search of the tower room uncovered a battered, leather scroll case. Gerhart snatched up as many of the handwritten notes as he could find, stuffing them hurriedly into the case, until the flames began to lick around the legs of the desk.

Then, stumbling through the flames, the fire hissing as if in frustration as it came into contact with his sodden robes, Gerhart made his flight from the observatory. He lurched down the worn steps of the spiralling stone staircase and out into the wind and rain of the unforgiving storm.

Behind the fleeing wizard the observatory resembled a beacon blazing on the desolate moors.

'AND YOU SAY this was all caused by one man?' the witch hunter asked, fixing the self-appointed village headman, Gustav Rothaarig, with a steely gaze from beneath the brim of his tall black hat.

'Pretty much,' the thickset, ginger-bearded man replied. 'The beast did some of the damage but it was the wizard who burnt the place.' The man spat the word 'wizard' as if it were venom.

The witch hunter Gottfried Verdammen surveyed the fire-blackened ruins of the village of Keulerdorf. The gloom of the fully overcast sky only added to the gloom of the village's inhabitants. The fire that had raged the previous week had damaged at least half the buildings. At best their walls and thatch had been scorched and blackened; at worst buildings had been razed to the ground – as had the village's stone-built hall.

As he surveyed the destruction, the witch hunter and his party remained silent. The witch hunter was dressed in practical black travelling clothes and boots. His black hat bore a leather band around it and a gleaming silver buckle above the brim. The only piece of his garb that was not black was his padded leather jerkin, in which, between layers of quilting, a series of iron plates had been stitched. It provided him with surprisingly effective armour. At his waist, and hanging from his belt, he wore a sabre and a holstered silver-metalled flintlock pistol. His heavy leather-gloved hands rested firmly on his hips in bunched fists.

The five men who made up his party were dressed in a similar manner. Gustav Rothaarig and the other villagers would have doubtless referred to them as zealots. The people of Keulerdorf put their trust in Sigmar, the Empire's patron, but only as much as they remembered the other older gods, such as Taal, god of nature, or Ulric, the ferocious, battling god of winter. For both the natural world and the seasons had greater immediate influence over the village folk of wooded and hilly Ostland than the Heldenhammer.

The men were rough looking individuals, unshaven and wild haired, quite in contrast to the black-clad Verdammen. Between them they appeared to be armed as heavily as a unit of free company fighters with bandoliers of daggers, swords and crossbows at their disposal. Every man wore some votive symbol of Lord Sigmar, whether it was a golden warhammer amulet about his neck or the crest of a twin-tailed comet stitched upon the front of his robes. Other, less conventional, lucky charms hung from wrist-bands and clothes, and one man even had what looked like a shrivelled claw hanging from a pin through a half-missing ear.

A slavering, straining bullmastiff, its coat black like its master's, was being held back by a scar-faced, heavily muscled zealot. He was attached to a chain hooked through the warhound's spiked collar. Behind the dog and its handler, another follower, whose nose had obviously been broken more than once in his eventful life, was holding the reins of the party's horses.

It was immediately apparent which steed belonged to Verdammen: it was the largest of the group's mounts, a black stallion with a white star emblazoned on its head. It wore a richly padded and stitched saddle on its back.

The usually more talkative Gustav was obviously becoming uncomfortable with the silence, and the forbidding presence of the witch hunter. 'The roof beams of the tithe barn were still smouldering only a few days ago and that was days since the maniac left,' he said.

'Indeed,' Verdammen answered coolly, tugging on the tails of his padded leather jerkin, realising that the man obviously expected some kind of response to his comment.

Over to the east lightning burst over the line of distant hills on the horizon. Beyond the foothills of the snow-capped Middle Mountains, in whose shadows Keulerdorf lay, a storm had broken with the violence of all-out war, judging by the echoes of thunder rolling over the darkly wooded uplands towards them.

Such dramatic and unseasonable weather had been on the increase over the months since the year turned. In fact, Verdammen recalled that it had begun when omens and portents were witnessed throughout the many lands of the Empire. Most terrifying and forbidding of all of them, however, had been the twin-tailed comet that had been seen streaking through the heavens. Rumour had spread like wildfire that all manner of horrors had occurred in its wake.

It was then that Gottfried Verdammen had been called upon by his covert masters in the Church of

Sigmar to take part in a most secret and unusual mission. He was to be one of the church's envoys to the Imperial colleges of magic, to join a clandestine kommission to investigate disturbances occurring in the north. His contact and counterpart among the wizard community was a celestial wizard whose studies had detected disturbances in what were commonly referred to, as the winds of magic. He was Kozma Himmlisch.

At the same time their kommission was to investigate the rise in random incidences of the influence of the dark forces of Chaos. Verdammen had been made aware by his superiors of many examples of Chaos mutation among the general populace. This had been accompanied by an increase in attacks by beastmen in the wilder parts of the Empire. So, for the last few months, Verdammen and Himmlisch had pursued their own, differing courses of action to see if there was a connection between these occurrences. Other unknown parties across the Empire did the same.

Verdammen was naturally suspicious of all magic. In fact he harboured an intense loathing of it, for he knew what many among the disparate population of the Empire did not. He had known ever since his father had sat him on his knee as a child and told him what a witch hunter needed to know. Verdammen's path had been clear from an early age: he would follow in the footsteps of his father, and all the generations before him. From birth it had been ordained that he would become a Templar fighting under the banner of Sigmar Heldenhammer, bringing the God-emperor's divine retribution upon all who dishonoured His hallowed name with unholy practices.

All magic came from Chaos and ultimately it would lead back to Chaos.

Gottfried distrusted and hated all practitioners of magic, but he was no fool, however. He understood that magic was a power that, like any other, could be used for good as well as evil, and that in the fight against Chaos, a servant of the forces of order needed to make use of every available weapon.

So it was that he was prepared to deal with wizards and their ilk. His party had been on their way to meet Verdammen's contact, Himmlisch, once again. The latter had investigated the curious birthings that had plagued the farming hamlet of Bauerzinnt that spring. He, however, would always rely on his faith in Sigmar, and his flintlock pistol, to fight evil.

As far as Verdammen was concerned, the rise in the power of Chaos in the world was in no small part due to the practices of 'rogue' wizards, unscrupulous individuals not properly regulated by the colleges of magic in Altdorf, who wandered the Empire unchecked. He had hunted down a number of spell-weavers in his time as a Templar of Sigmar: they were foul Chaos cultists and morbid, grave-robbing necromancers on the whole, so he put them to death. They were a blot upon the face of the world that had to be removed.

'You are certain that this was the work of one man?' Verdammen pressed.

'I saw it with my own eyes,' Gustav replied, soundly vexed.

'But there are still some things I am uncertain about,' the witch hunter went on. 'I have a few more questions.'

· After almost half an hour of questioning the talkative villager fell silent.

'Schultz,' Verdammen said at last, beckoning to the man minding the horses. 'We have seen all we need to here.'

The witch hunter's party began to mount up as Schultz led the stallion over to Verdammen, who was still incredulous at the devastation one unruly spellcaster could cause.

'You're leaving?' Gustav asked, with barely suppressed relief.

'Who did this to your village?' the witch hunter asked as he put a foot in a stirrup and climbed into the saddle.

'I already told you!' the headman snapped. 'It was a wizard. He was ten feet tall with eyes like burning coals. A devil from the depths of hell.'

Gustav hawked a gob of phlegm and spat it at the ground, muttering half under his breath, 'Filthy vagabond mage. Spawn of the Dark Powers the lot of them.'

'But you have not told me his name. Do you know what it was?' Verdammen asked, his voice measured and calm as a man on the verge of losing his patience.

'No, I don't know his name,' the headman said sourly, afraid that the unremitting questioning was about to begin again. Gustav met the witch hunter's gaze. 'It's probably something that can only be spoken in the twisted tongue of the Dark Powers anyway.'

The witch hunter jerked his horse's reins, turning him towards the east.

'What will you do now? Are you going to go after the wizard?' Gustav asked, his voice tired and strained.

'In time, when I am ready,' Verdammen confirmed and, kicking his heels into the stallion's flanks, led his band of zealots out of the village.

Gottfried Verdammen would indeed hunt down the mage responsible for the razing of Keulerdorf, but first he had a prior appointment to keep. No doubt Kozma Himmlisch would be waiting for him, eager to tell him what more he had scryed from the movements of the stars and the winds of magic that swept around his lonely tower.

For the time being the pyromaniac fire mage would have to wait.

TWO
Dead and Buried

'Those who would accuse me of necromancy know not of what they speak. It is true that the Wind of Shyish is drawn to places of death, and doom follows in its wake, but I am no corpse-lover. And if any man makes such an accusation again he will learn that it does not do to trouble a wizard of the lore of death.'

– Todende Sterbefall, Grand Warlock of the Amethyst order, before the purging of Grabmalholz

THE WARRIOR PRIEST looked down on the huddle of stone buildings clustered around the aged stone bridge at the foot of the valley. He could see precious few signs that there was any life in this place. There was no one outside in the streets. There were no domestic animals visible in the pens outside some of the dwellings. Thin wisps of smoke rose from a few chimney stacks. Under the uniform overcast sky of late afternoon the houses seemed the colour of tombstones.

So this was Steinbrucke, the priest thought. A small unassuming village at the heart of the principality of Ostland, several leagues from the nearest town. There had been a settlement here since the Unberogen tribe first settled these lands.

The village had grown around a fording place on the River Wasche. In time the stone bridge had been built to provide a more practical means for travellers and merchant wagons to cross the river on the road towards Wolfenburg. The people of Steinbrucke made their living from the Wasche itself, as well as the passing trade that the river crossing brought their way. There might only be one mill in the village but there was also a coaching inn, a blacksmith's, a carter's and a wheelwright's.

But none of this made Steinbrucke unusual. What had drawn the priest here were the rumours. Sinister news had a habit of travelling far and wide and there was no one more likely to hear it than a martyr in search of a mission. At least that was what some would call him: Lector Wilhelm Faustus simply saw himself as a loyal servant of Sigmar doing his lord's holy work as best he could.

When he had heard that the congregation of Steinbrucke had lost their faith in Lord Sigmar, and that as a consequence the powers of darkness had shown their hand, he knew he had to intervene.

Sitting in the saddle of his great grey steed – a warhorse to rival those of the gallant knights of Bretonnia – stark against the horizon at the crest of the valley, Wilhelm Faustus was an imposing presence. He wore a cowled cloak, like a monk's, over his armoured upper body. From the waist down he wore a skirt of chain mail, heavy britches and sturdy leather boots. His hands were gauntleted. In the left he held his heavy-headed warhammer and on his right arm rested a battered shield, bearing the device of Sigmar's comet but with an iron skull at its core.

But the most distinctive things about him were his gleaming bald head and the book of holy litany transcribed from the *Book of Sigmar* that was bound to his forehead by a strap of leather. For Wilhelm believed that if the first thing in his mind was his devotion for his Lord Sigmar then nothing ill could befall him. He also carried a copy of the complete *Book of Sigmar*, bound in iron covered with a tracery of fine metals.

His down-turned features were also marked by a cruel scar that described a path from the top of his head, across his left eye, down his cheek and twisted across the lips of his tight-drawn mouth.

His horse was no less imposing. Hanging from its harness were several macabre trophies. The most recently taken was the still-bloody malformed, tusked head of a green-skinned orc. The other three were skulls, the flesh and hair having been boiled from them to leave nothing but gleaming, off-white bone. The largest was caprine in form with curling ram's horns. The other two appeared to be human: on the cranium of one the word 'Heretic' had been etched in a pronounced gothic hand; the other bore the title 'Damnatus' and appeared to have particularly elongated incisors. These were all evidence of Wilhelm's fight against the followers of evil, and his victories.

For that was what it meant to be a warrior priest of Sigmar. To be a man of action as well as a man of words. To be adept in the martial skills of the warhammer, and other such weapons, and to be just as well versed in the holy scriptures and devotional prayers of the Sigmarite order. To practise abstinence, to keep the body strong and the spirit pure in the battle against the powers of darkness. To go out into the world to rid it of malefactors, blasphemers and Chaos-worshippers, even though the odds may at first seem insurmountable. To be firm in the belief that faith alone could conquer evil. That was what it meant to be a warrior priest.

Wilhelm Faustus had first heard the call to fight for Sigmar decades before. But he had heard the call anew only a matter of months ago, at the turning of the year recorded in the Imperial record as 2521.

In fact, if people had had the eyes to see it, it would have been witnessed throughout the Empire. It had been present in all the dark and ominous portents that were seen across the countryside and in the towns as well, from Hochsleben and Wissenburg to Salzenmund and Bechafen. The message could not have been clearer: the Heldenhammer asked that those who still held their faith fight back against the rise in Chaos, and hold back the tide of evil that threatened to sweep through the lands.

So it was that the warrior priest had readied his horse Kreuz, and packed for a long journey. He was to set off for the lands that lay under the shadow of the north. Lector Wilhelm Faustus's holy destiny lay, he believed, in him taking the fight against evil unto the very wastes of Chaos.

Of course, as he travelled ever northwards through the blighted baronies and principalities of the Empire, he saw corruption and heresy all around him. His own religious fervour would not let him merely stand by and ignore the servants of the Dark Powers that worked their evil in the communities of the good people. As a consequence, his travels had been interrupted on many occasions as he saw to the spiritual and physical needs of Sigmar's people. Sometimes he had worked alone and sometimes others had assisted him in his holy labour.

And so he had returned to Steinbrucke and the curse their village was under. The villagers might have once been counted among the good people of the Empire but they had allowed their faith to wane. Rather than seeing the call of their god to take up arms against the visions and signs abroad throughout the land, the villagers of Steinbrucke had only seen the collapse of what little civilisation remained in their part of the world.

If such a lapse of faith was allowed to continue it could spread and grow like a canker, and corrupt the very heart of the Empire. And it could spell the downfall of the rule of the Emperor Karl-Franz and his noble upstanding elector counts.

But it was not Wilhelm's way to punish the guilty by doing away with the innocent. The people's lack of faith was like an illness, to be purged from them. They needed a demonstration of the power of Sigmar for all its god-emperor's awe-inspiring glory. In time he hoped such an approach would have satisfying consequences for the Empire and its loyal subjects.

And if the rumours, which had led him to Steinbrucke were to be believed, such a demonstration would not be hard to arrange. For it was said that foul things had been seen lumbering through the fields at night and unearthly moans broke the peace of night time slumbers. Unnatural powers were at work in this place.

He had first heard talk of the village in the taproom of The Goat's Head in Hirschalle. He heard of the inhabitants' fear and faithlessness and the powers of darkness that had taken hold, drawing doom-loving essences to its lands. In Galgenbaum he had heard that the village of Steinbrucke was now shunned by all but the most implacable or desperate travellers. Apparently there had not been a priest there for some months. At night the people hid behind their sturdy stone walls whilst the dead expelled from the earth by the dark power walked the streets and tried to reclaim the homes that had once been theirs.

With these thoughts, Wilhelm urged Kreuz forward and began to descend the track that led to the ancient stone bridge and the cowering village beyond. His horse's iron-shod hooves clacked on the flinty track, and his trophies rattled on the harness.

A light rain had begun to fall and there was a distinctly un-springlike chill in the air. Wilhelm pulled his cowl over his head, throwing the grim features of his face into shadow. He appeared sinister, like some prophet of the End Times.

As he entered the village, feeling the rain pattering his bald head through the fabric of his hood, Wilhelm was greeted by a succession of doors and shutters being slammed firmly shut. Was this welcome just for him or was it in part because dusk was falling and the dark things were about to approach?

The lector realised that, if nothing else, the slamming doors were a sign that he was not welcome here. After all, the people of Steinbrucke had long ago abandoned any notion that the priesthood of Sigmar could assist them. He had come to this place uninvited and if he had any sense he would ride straight through and find shelter elsewhere before nightfall. Whatever might befall him if he chose to remain was none of the villagers' concern; he had brought it upon himself.

The settlement, which looked as if it had once been reasonably well-to-do, appeared to have fallen on harder times in recent months.

Wilhelm had already seen how poorly tended and weed-choked the fields beyond the village had become. Many of the buildings were also beginning to show signs of neglect. Wilhelm noticed that some hasty repairs had been made to missing tiles on the roofs of the houses and saw strange scratches on many of the now closed doors and window shutters, which looked suspiciously like claw marks.

But it was the establishments that had previously relied on passing trade that showed the worst neglect and disrepair. The paintwork on the frontage of the inn was faded and peeling, and the drinking house did not even seem to be open. But then if, as Wilhelm now strongly suspected, the rumours he had heard about unnatural things infesting this place were true, then no one would want to be out after dark on any night, no matter what the weather.

The great wheel of the mill that stood at the edge of the village creaked mournfully as it rotated. It served no purpose now that the farmers took their precious harvests elsewhere.

'If you would save your village and yourselves,' Wilhelm called to the shadowy shapes of buildings around him, as if berating their occupants, 'then pray now to your saviour, Lord Sigmar himself!'

The rain continued to fall on Steinbrucke, puddles forming in the hoof-prints left by Kreuz's heavy tread. Through the drizzle the village looked even more dour and desolated. Wilhelm had thought he had seen the most neglected of Steinbrucke's properties and places until, guiding Kreuz between the homes and boarded-up businesses, he saw a smaller, low domed building at the edge of the village.

It was a chapel, its stonework cracked and crumbling. Ivy and lichen covered almost every square inch of the building. Surmounting the dome of the roof was a statue of a noble warrior holding a stone warhammer in his strong hands; it was doubtless meant to be an image of the Heldenhammer himself.

The door to the chapel and the few shallow steps leading up to it were choked with weeds. The carved faces of saints peered forlornly, with sadness in their stone eyes, from between the fronds of greenery that smothered the holy place.

Hot, righteous anger flared within Wilhelm. How could anyone have allowed such a thing to happen? For a moment he felt like abandoning Steinbrucke to its fate; they must have brought it upon themselves.

Then the priest took a deep breath, closed his eyes and cast a prayer to Sigmar, asking his forgiveness. No, he had come here to rid the village of whatever was plaguing it, and to prevent the powers of darkness from gaining further footholds in the blessed lands of the Empire.

Wilhelm dismounted. Having tied Kreuz's reins securely to a tree branch that hung over the wall of the cemetery, he gazed upon the derelict building in front of him, hefting his consecrated warhammer in his gauntleted hands.

Wilhem's warhammer was comprised of a shaft of wood, braced with iron. It was five spans long and surmounted with a heavy iron head. The otherwise flat hammer-face was studded with brutal spikes, and inscribed on one side with a curling 'S' that was set within a representation of a twin-tailed comet. The end of the warhammer was bound with leather and culminated in a loop of chain. Feeling the weapon's reassuring weight in his hands, the priest walked purposefully towards the chapel.

As the last light seeped from the sky above the rim of the valley, Wilhelm could just make out the shadows of broken tombstones in the graveyard – crooked black shapes just darker than the land from which they rose. His eyes steadily adjusted to the deepening darkness. The only sounds were those of the rain pattering down around him and the eerie keening of a light breeze as it blew through the branches of the yews trees around the edge of the graveyard.

Reaching the top of the chapel steps, Wilhelm cautiously pushed open the door with the head of his hammer. All that met him was a deep darkness.

Closing his eyes again and focussing his mind as if in a state of meditation, Wilhelm prayed to Sigmar to aid him in his task to purge Steinbrucke of evil. Returning to his steed beside the cemetery wall, Wilhelm unpacked a lantern from the horse's saddlebags. Once the lantern was lit, he braved the shrine. The warm, golden glow banished the creeping shadows from the interior of the neglected chapel.

Then he heard it: a skittering of loose earth and stones, and the eerie keening of the wind that sounded like moaning. Wilhelm turned from the chapel door and raising the glowing head of his warhammer above him, peered into the cemetery beyond.

At first he could see nothing between the broken tombstones and the occasional age-cracked crypt. Then, out of the corner of his eye, he caught a glimpse of shifting soil. Immediately focussing on the spot, Wilhelm saw something push itself free of the disturbed ground. Five, thin nubs of bone appeared, followed by the gleaming dome of a skull.

The warrior priest could feel his heart beating against his ribs but he consciously kept his breathing deep and slow, channelling the adrenaline now rushing through his system. He was readying himself to act calmly, rather than letting the foe force him into careless action.

This was not the first time he had witnessed the dead rise from their graves. He had been party to all manner of disturbing and supernatural phenomena in his quest to bring the holy light of Sigmar to the darkest corners of the Empire.

The human skeleton, its bones held together by strips of rotted muscle and leathery sinews, struggled free of its grave and rose into a hunched stoop. After a moment's pause, whilst the bony silhouette swayed disconcertingly from side to side as if it were finding its balance, the animated human remains crept unerringly towards the lector. Its movements were insect-like and unsettling.

Wilhelm was now aware of the sound of other bodies pulling themselves free of the tainted ground. Swinging his glowing warhammer around and above him, Wilhelm caught glimpses of age-yellowed bone, grave-soil smeared pallid skin, grey-green flesh, clumps of matted hair peeling from bloodless scalps and decomposing faces distended by slack-jawed moaning mouths. They were all stalking and stumbling towards him.

Now was the time to act!

Gripping the warhammer firmly in both hands Wilhelm felt the muscles in his arms bunch as his legs propelled him towards the rising revenants. Closing the distance between himself and the risen corpses, Wilhelm swung with his weapon. The hammerhead connected with the grey skull of the first skeleton, exploding its cranium into shards of bone as it was knocked clean from the vertebrae of its neck. What remained of the skeleton took a few more unsteady staggering steps before Wilhelm's counter swing quite literally took its legs from under it. The bones clattered onto a fallen, lichen-stained headstone, the ribcage coming to rest amidst a thicket of thistles.

Night had fallen completely, and the rain began to pelt down more heavily than before. Unperturbed, the revenants continued to pull themselves free of the dampening ground, and advanced towards the warrior priest, slipping drunkenly through the mud.

Adrenaline filled Wilhelm with religious fervour. He continued to lay about him, smiting the undead before they could get their filthy, clawing talons within reach of him. The warhammer glowed more brightly every time it connected with a corpse, shattering bones and pulverising partially decomposed flesh under its blows.

But the number of the revenants was steadily increasing and, although they did not move quickly, they were slowly but surely closing in on Wilhelm, eventually trapping him between the crush of their bodies. As he backhanded a stinking cadaver that was chattering the broken stumps of its teeth at him incessantly, the priest felt something scrabbling at his boots. He kicked out and was dimly aware of a wet splintering sound as his foot connected brutally with something at ground level.

Splintered bony talons scraped across the metal of Wilhelm's breastplate and snagged against the straps and buckles holding it in place. The priest kicked out again, knocking the fleshless husk of a corpse far enough away to take a swing at it with his hammer. The weapon shattered its ribcage and backbone before it pulverised the face of a green-tinged flailing zombie. Decomposing grey matter spurted from the newly opened cracks in its skull.

There were too many of them, and they were getting too close. He was outnumbered by more than twenty to one, he guessed. The undead were relentless, never tiring, and where one fell, three more were already pulling themselves free of the mouldering earth to take its place. They did not feel pain and fought on even when they had sustained injuries that would have felled a living creature. In fact, their unremitting attacks were too much for one man.

But Lector Wilhelm Faustus was not just any man. He was a man of god and with his faith in Sigmar he would overcome these spawn of evil.

Driven into a state of furious ecstasy, Wilhelm called on his god to intervene again. He could feel every fibre of his body being charged with the divine power of the Heldenhammer. A warm golden glow suffused every part of him. He felt as if he was surrounded by a halo of golden, shimmering light.

There was a moment's silence and then a burst of sound like a roaring fire that swallowed all noise before it. Energy erupted from the warrior priest in an explosion of brilliantly bright blazing light, and it lit the graveyard with its incandescence. Raindrops hissed, evaporated by the heat blast.

The sound of the wind in the yew trees returned in an even more agonised howl as the bodies of the dead were blasted apart by the sheer physical force of Wilhelm's faith. Rotten flesh melted and sloughed from bones in the face of the explosion. Parchment-dry skin burst into flame. Mouldering bones clattered against the side of the chapel as soul fire ripped through the pack of undead.

The echoes of the explosion of retribution died and the sounds of the night returned. Wilhelm's skin was a mass of gooseflesh and his muscles tingled with the power that had been channelled through him. He gazed upon the broken stones of the cemetery that were now littered with the charred and bubbling remains of the undead.

Then he heard it again: the skittering of shifting soil, the hollow tap and scrape of naked bone against granite, the splintering of rotten coffin wood. The dead certainly did not rest easily in Steinbrucke.

Wilhelm felt exhausted, the drawn-out battle and expulsion of holy energy had drained his vital strength. Yet despite feeling the strain, the priest prepared to fight on regardless and hastily muttered another prayer to Sigmar.

He straightened his breastplate and shook coffin-dirt from his monk's robe. Then he drew his hood tight about his head again before hefting his warhammer in both hands and striding further into the cursed graveyard.

He would not rest until every last one of the corpses advancing towards him over the sodden ground was dead and buried for ever.

GOTTFRIED VERDAMMEN SURVEYED the smouldering ruins of the tower, a look of grim resignation in his steely eyes. The Tower of Heaven had once stood at the top of this crag overlooking the rushing rapids of the unnamed tributary below. It had been the highest point of land for leagues around, before the roots of the Middle Mountains rose leagues away to the west. It had stood one hundred feet tall, isolated and remote: the ideal location for a sorcerer like Kozma Himmlisch to practise his mysterious art. And now it was nothing more than blackened rubble.

Fire had ravaged the structure. The conflagration must have been furious and intense: the interior of the tower had been gutted and its foundation stones cracked, so that the astromancer's ancient home had collapsed utterly.

Cold fury simmered beneath the surface of Verdammen's coldly calculating mind. It seemed that the rising tide of Chaos was determined to thwart them at every turn. The witch hunter did not rate his chances of finding the celestial wizard alive as being very good.

The rest of the witch hunter's party began to search the tumble of masonry, the mastiff straining on the end of its chain-leash as it sniffed through the debris for any bodies. Verdammen himself could see the twisted metal corpse of the colossal telescope amongst the masonry; a paradigm of some sorcerer-scientist's art now destroyed forever.

His party had travelled for five days since leaving Keulerdorf. They had ridden in the face of relentless wind and rain through the wilds of Ostland, over rocky hills, between the cathedral-pillar trunks of twisted, brooding woodland and across the bleak wind-swept emerald-black moors until they had reached the Tower of Heaven.

At least the rain seemed to have subsided. This morning had been the first to dawn for a week without a blustery shower. It still didn't feel like spring, though.

Verdammen was shaken from his reverie by the warhound's strident barking.

'Herr Verdammen!' the scar-faced Gunther called from the shattered remains of an arched window. 'The dog's found something!'

The witch hunter hastily made his way to his associate. The mastiff was straining on its chain as it scrabbled and worried at something buried under the blackened timbers and fire-cracked stones. Gunther held the slavering animal back as Verdammen heaved a charred beam free.

There, at the centre of a blackened patch of ground, which the rain had turned into ashy mud, was a blackened corpse, transfixed by a twisted and melted spear of metal.

'Is it him?' Gunther asked aghast. 'Is it the astromancer?'

The burnt body was unrecognisable. No hair remained on its scorched skull and the clothes had either burned away completely or had been fused with the melted flesh. There was one identifying mark, however.

Around the withered and blistered neck of the corpse hung the liquefied remains of a chain bearing a medallion. The fire had been hot enough to begin to melt the symbol but it had not been enough to destroy it utterly. To anyone else the markings on the talisman might have meant nothing, but to a fellow member of the kommission of the colleges of magic they were immediately recognisable. And Verdammen wore an identical medallion himself.

'Indeed. It is Kozma Himmlisch,' the witch hunter said plainly.

The zealot was happy to take his master's word for it and did not question how he knew. It was enough that the witch hunter said it was the case.

Verdammen considered the body of the celestial wizard with thoughtful detachment. Although the astromancer's death hampered his investigations somewhat, Himmlisch could have expected little else. For, from the witch hunter's experience, a violent death was the fate that awaited all those who dealt in sorcery. Their dabblings in the art caught up with them in the end, whether their use of such power corrupted them beyond redemption or proved too formidable for them to control. Ultimately, they all damned themselves.

And talking of fire, the devastation here had all the hallmarks of the devastation Verdammen had seen in Keulerdorf: a building savagely destroyed by flames.

Was it possible, Verdammen wondered, that the wizard the villagers had spoken of in Keulerdorf had been here before them and that for the last five days the witch hunter's party had already unwittingly been tracking him? All he needed now was some evidence.

His eyes scouring every nook and cranny between the broken and burnt masonry, Verdammen began a frantic search of the ruins. He needed a sign that the fire wizard had been involved in the death of Kozma

Himmlisch and the razing of the Tower of Heaven, and some clue as to the pyromancer's identity. And then, in no time at all, as if he were meant to find it, there was all the evidence he needed, lying there in front of him, half-buried in the mud and ash.

It was a key. A golden key. His eye had been drawn to it by the gleam of the yellow metal amongst the blackened mess.

Picking the key up, he rubbed it clean of muck and held it up for his henchmen to see. The zealots had all crowded around him with the discovery of the wizard's body.

'It's a key,' one of them stated, the slow tone of his voice denoting his blissful lack of intelligence.

'Not just any key,' Verdammen said, studying the object in minute detail. 'I'll wager that this key did not open a single lock in this tower.'

The artefact was no more than a stylised representation of a key and certainly bore no scratch marks, as one would expect of a key that had been used as one. The witch hunter had seen other such keys before and he strongly suspected this one was the same as the others: golden keys of office among the Bright order of the colleges of magic in distant Altdorf.

It was the evidence the suspicious witch hunter needed. A wizard of the Bright order had been here who had already run riot within these forsaken lands. The pyromancer had gone too far, his terrible powers now controlled him. Verdammen had seen it happen on too many occasions before. This man, this pawn of the Dark Powers, had succumbed to the corrupting control of Chaos and embraced the blasphemous powers of evil. And he was still on the loose. He was an out of control killer who could be trusted to fight for justice, righteousness and the living Emperor Karl-Franz no longer. The sorcerer had become a murderer, and it was Verdammen's place to stop him.

So this would now become the witch hunter's mission. In that instant Verdammen determined to hunt down the bright wizard Gerhart Brennend and bring an end to his murderous rampage.

THREE
The Leper of Grunhafen

'When the ravages of age and disease take their toll, when harvests are blighted and famine threatens, that is when desperate men – men without hope – make supplication to the Grandfather to stay his scabrous hand. And it is from that moment that they are damned.'

– A Treatise Upon the Nature of the
Fell Powers,
by Brother-Scrivener Schreiber

IT HAD BEEN a week now since Gerhart Brennend had escaped the destruction of the tower-observatory of Kozma Himmlisch, and he was still walking through the highlands of Ostland under a permanently dark, overcast sky. There was little difference between day and night, so heavily smothered by

47

cloud was the vast expanse of sky. And still it rained.

He was cold, wet, tired and hungry as he had never been before. He looked dishevelled and unwell, the lack of proper food and shelter taking their toll on him.

Since his battle with the astromancer Gerhart had not seen hide or hair of another human soul. The marshes of Ostland were as wild and untamed a place as any within the broad boundaries of the Empire. Herds of beastmen and goblin tribes lurked within the feral depths of the Forest of Shadows, as they did within the bramble-strangled, twisted heart of the more notorious Drakwald to the south.

The treacherous passes of the mountains were a sanctuary for human renegades and the followers of proscribed cults, as well as trolls, giants and worse. Gerhart had discovered this for himself at Keulerdorf. Then there were the raids of the Norse to contend with, marauding orcs and even, on occasion, bloodthirsty forays made by Kislevite bandits.

Of course, lying so close to the north-eastern border of the Empire, the Elector Counts of Ostland had fought alongside the hard-bitten warriors of the frozen tundra land of Kislev in their mutual cause to prevent the forces of Chaos rampaging south. However, if the astromancer's speculations were accurate, it would seem that soon the whole of the Old World would be playing host to an invasion the likes of which had not been seen in five hundred years. All the armies of Ostland and Kislev would have difficulty containing it, let alone holding it back.

The Emperor on his throne in Altdorf, or the Elector Count of Ostland, Valmir von Raukov, bearer of one of the Runefang blades of legend, secure within his castle in the grand principality's capital of Wolfenburg, might claim that these lands were civilised. But both men, 'heroes in their own right', had fought long and hard in defence of these northern lands.

Civilisation only really existed in these lands as a concept. Certainly armies could be mustered from among the vassal subjects of the Empire's many states and cities to repel invaders and quash rebellions. Trade took place between the different regions on a fairly regular basis, with losses expected in these wild and dangerous times. Barges carried cargoes along the river ways of the Empire to the great free port of Marienburg and beyond to the chivalrous lands of Bretonnia and the city-states of Tilea as far as the coast of dusty Araby. The cities of the Empire were renowned as great centres of learning, where the secrets of alchemy and magic were plumbed alongside new advances in metallurgy, munitions and steam-locomotion.

Yet despite all of these great achievements the truth of the matter was that much of the countryside beyond the patrolled highways and the ancient cities was actually a dangerous wilderness of brooding, unruly forests, craggy, wind-scoured uplands and desolate moors divided by rushing rivers. People hid inside their cities, towns and villages, protected by thick stone walls and tall stockades, or in their castles, and the majority never ventured further than a few miles from their homes in their lifetime.

But the time was coming when perhaps not even such fastnesses of ancient strength would be safe from the storm rising in the north.

It was only now, as Gerhart descended from the highlands that eventually rose up to meet the Middle Mountains behind him to the west that Gerhart saw more regular signs of human habitation once again.

In truth Gerhart had encountered some already on his travels, signs that in remote places these lands had once been inhabited. Ancient barrow-mounds and weather worn stone circles, uncorrupted by the sigils of Dark Gods or their followers, the shells of abandoned farmsteads reclaimed by nature and turf covered mounds that suggested that once a settlement had stood here.

At least these abandoned habitations had provided him with some respite from the incessant rain and a place to sleep. He had spent one night in the shelter of a decrepit windmill and another under the roof of a vacant shepherd's hovel, listening to the deluge pounding against the rotting thatch above his head.

The rest of the time he had had to make do sheltering between the towering boulders on hilltops or crawling into shallow caves, having checked that there was nothing else living there first. Then, alone and undisturbed, the wizard had focussed his mind. He saw the winds of magic as their breezes danced over the rain-drenched land, reaching out to capture a strand of fiery power, the essence of Aqshy. It had been enough to start a small fire with which to warm himself, heat through some provisions and dry out his soaking clothes.

In the light of the fire, Gerhart had been able to go through the random notes he had taken from Kozma's observatory. He wanted to make sense of the astromancer's urgent scribblings. He was aware that the jottings were the ramblings of an unsound mind, but they kept coming back to the same conclusion. It had taken Gerhart some time but thanks to information he had gleaned himself before encountering Kozma Himmlisch, he had gradually been able to work out the gist of the astromancer's observations.

Using his arcane telescope, the celestial wizard had spent months observing the the flow of the winds of magic, and the heavens over the lands that lay to the extreme north. Kozma Himmlisch had suspected a rise in the power of Chaos, as the expanse of land covered by the warping Shadow increased, like a beach being swallowed by the high tide.

This ebb and flow of dark power, just like the waxing and waning of the moons, was not unusual. Those who knew about such things realised that it happened every year with the passing of the seasons. But those same people, would also have realised, as Gerhart had, that this current swelling of the Shadow was unprecedented in recent history. At best it would pass slowly. At worst it might swallow the entire world.

To Gerhart, this all seemed the conjecture of an unsound mind, but of one thing he was certain, that this rise of power in the north, like a storm of Chaos building on the borders of the lands of men, could threaten the whole Empire.

So he was now striding north himself, walking the highways and the byways of Ostland, using his oak staff to aid him. For, even if he ended up having to face all the multitudinous hordes of the north alone, he had to do what he could to atone for his sins.

Ahead of him lay the sentinel city of Wolfenburg and no doubt the greatest challenge he had faced in all his forty-five years of life, if Kozma's ramblings were to be believed.

The pieces of parchment that bore Kozma Himm-lisch's forbidding divinations were stowed inside his robes, crumpled and water-stained, even though Gerhart had done his best to keep them dry. After all, they were the only proof he had of what he had seen and what he now furiously believed.

As the turf squelched underfoot, Gerhart guessed he had covered a fair bit of ground since leaving the burning tower behind. The leather of his boots was stained and discoloured from the perpetual wet and splashing mud. With only a hint of the sun behind a slight lightening of the constant grey cloud cover, Gerhart could nevertheless see that the track he was on showed signs of greater use and was descending steadily towards a wooded valley.

And then he glimpsed the smoke rising through the mist and rain, still some miles ahead of him at the limit of his vision in this miserable weather. But before he reached the source of the smoke, Gerhart came upon the first of the deserted villages.

THE STILLNESS WAS unsettling. The only sounds Ger-hart was aware of, as he cautiously made his way towards the crossroads around which a few stone, timber and thatch buildings were clustered, were those that he himself made or those of the remorse-less wind and rain. An air of death hung over the village like a burial shroud. There were no signs of life at all, human or otherwise. But then that was hardly surprising given the apparent fate of the settlement.

On every hovel door Gerhart could see a cross, daubed in thick red paint. This was a common practice in the northern lands of the Empire when dire circumstances struck. Some of these same doors, along with windows and any other entrance to the buildings had been boarded up and nailed shut from the outside.

It was a sign that spoke of a long and lingering death. It spoke of plague.

Wherever a cross had been painted, it told a tragic tale of entire families being boarded up inside their homes, abandoned by their neighbours. Even if only one family member succumbed to the sickness, every last inhabitant of the house would be trapped inside with the plague victim, condemned to infection and inevitable death, either from the illness, starvation, or at their own hands – trying to save themselves from the suffering that was sure to follow.

People who had once regarded each other as friends were now shut away. Friendships were forgotten, familial ties severed, and kind-hearted neighbours became compassionless pragmatists as they consigned those infected to a terrible fate.

For there was no room for compassion when it came to the plague. It simply had to be contained. A small hamlet or village already infected could hardly hope to survive at all if the spread of the disease was not caught in time. So the villagers put themselves into self-imposed quarantine and prayed to whatever beneficent god might be listening to save them in their most desperate hour.

Should they not do so, and one of the roving bands of Sigmarite Templars discover them, then their fate was assured; they faced death by sword and fire, possibly following a painful and unnecessary inquisition.

How had it begun, Gerhart wondered? A polluted water supply? A hex cast upon these poor common folk? An illness borne by rats, possibly even the product of the foul machinations of the rat-kin?

And how had it been spread? By an infected cargo brought by wagon to the village? A passing peddler? Intentionally by those corrupted of mind, as well as body, by the disease to serve the blasphemous powers ranged against mankind?

How long had it been since this anonymous village had succumbed to the plague, its name dying along with the last person to ever know it?

Gerhart did not break open any of the doors to discover what lay within. He already knew what he would find and, besides, he had probably seen worse fighting alongside the armies of Empire. There was nothing he could do for the people who had lived here except purge the place with purifying fire.

Concentrating his mind, Gerhart reached out and called the winds of magic to him. The tip of his staff sparked then burst into flames. He walked round the village, igniting the thatches of the forsaken homes, turning them into fiery sepulchres. Despite the endless rain, the wizard found the thatches to be dry under the eaves and there the fires took.

Gerhart left the hamlet with the buildings behind him ablaze. Thick grey smoke swelled from their thatches, and tall flames licked up the walls, consuming everything in their insatiable hunger.

At the next settlement, less than half a league away the story was the same. The same miasma of death hung over the stockaded village, the same red crosses daubed on the walls and doors, silence instead of birdsong. There were no signs of life at all. Once again he could do no more than put the place to the torch. With the power of Chaos building on the northern borders of the Empire, he had to cauterise the canker of evil growing within it.

So it continued. One hamlet after another, entire villages were wiped out, and lone farmsteads stood as silent as the grave. Forges, tanneries and even shrines, smeared with the same condemning crosses, all went up in smoke, purged with the same cleansing fire.

Had all of these settlements succumbed to the plague? There were no obvious signs that anything had been wrong in many of them. Gerhart had heard tales of whole villages being condemned to an untimely death by paranoia alone. If one man came down with a blood-fever or severe bout of stomach cramps, paranoia would do the rest, more often than not fuelled by religious fanatics and over enthusiastic witch hunters.

Days later, as he left another settlement to its fate amongst the flames, Gerhart turned and looked back at the path he had followed through the forest. Behind him black smoke rose from settlements he had put to the torch. It hung over the treetops in a pall, making it seem like Morr's own raven of death had descended from the shadowy, unreal realm beyond the veil to gather the souls released at last by the funeral pyres.

It soon transpired that Gerhart was not the only one seeking to purge the plague from the land. Two days later he encountered the doom-mongers of Sigmar.

HAVING SPENT THE previous night sleeping in the shelter of an ancient beech, a fair few miles from the last forester's hut he had put to the torch, Gerhart now found himself on a path that wound around the side of a hill covered with sycamores before dropping down into a shallow valley between four low hills. The village that lay nestled in the hollow was already partially obscured by the dirty grey smoke coiling from the bonfires smouldering all around it.

Through the smoky billows that drifted between the trunks of the trees Gerhart could see that a river meandered through the stockaded settlement. It wound through two wicker water gates, and a number of barges were moored at a jetty on the northern bank of the watercourse inside the village.

The wizard sniffed sharply, catching the acrid smell of burning on the breeze that drifted across the valley and rode over the rolling contours of the hills. It was said by doctors and those who made the study of the human body that smell was the most evocative of all the senses. Certainly that was how it affected Gerhart now. The scent of the bonfires made his heart race and he felt the warm glow of the esoteric wind of Aqshy pass through him. He could see the red vapours of the ethereal wind at the edge of his vision, following the path of the smoke through the trees.

But something else was carried to him on the wind, something that affected the wizard almost as strongly as the scent of burning: the cries, screams and prayers of desperate people, suffused with the shouts and invocations of their attackers.

Gerhart quickened his pace down the hillside.

Once he reached the outskirts of the village, he could see figures moving through the obscuring smoke. They were shadowy and indistinct, and although he could not make out the appearance of individuals he could read quite clearly what was going on by their desperate movements. Many were running in panic, others following on their heels with what appeared to be more measured steps.

Gerhart realised that the panicked villagers were being herded into the centre of the village to where another fire, larger than the others, was blazing.

The smoke drifting from the other conflagrations had at first hidden this fire from him. As another cloud of smoke drifted clear of the village Gerhart saw that part of the stockade enclosing the buildings had been uprooted to fuel the fire, along with the wood and straw pillaged from a ruined barn.

Gerhart guessed that the smaller bonfires burning on the outskirts of the village had been lit to purify the air of the invisible, malignant contagion that was the plague. But this much larger conflagration, burning at its heart, had a much more sinister purpose, he was sure.

Suddenly a woman ran across the space between two houses, her hair and torn dress flapping around her. She was pursued by a man wearing a monk-like habit who was waving a spike ended flail over his head.

Gerhart passed under a signpost, a plaque of wood hanging by chains creaking in the slight breeze. He looked up and read the name recorded

there in faded and peeled paint, in an angular
gothic hand: *Grunhafen*.

WITH NO ONE on guard at the southern gate leading
into Grunhafen, Gerhart was able to walk into the
village unhindered. He could hear the buzzing of
flies in the air. Figures ran towards him out of the
coiling smoke, gaunt faces distorted by screams,
streaming with tears of terror, or hidden by deep
hoods and sinister leather masks. Then they were
gone again, swallowed up by the thick bonfire
smoke.

One robed thickset man charged at him bellowing, but came to an abrupt halt as Gerhart swung his
staff sharply into his stomach. As the fanatic collapsed, winded, onto his knees, Gerhart saw quite
clearly the angular embroidered 'S' on the front of
his robes. It was the same with the others among the
pursuers. They were zealots; men of Sigmar.

'What is going on here?' the fire mage muttered.

Ignoring the cat and mouse games of the villagers
and their aggressors, Gerhart strode into the all-
enveloping acrid clouds, making his way towards
the centre of the village. It was there, he was certain,
that his questions would be answered.

The darker grey shapes of gable-ends loomed at
him out of the murk, increasing the sense of claus-
trophobia that the choking smoke had already laid
over the place. Then the shadowy ghosts of the
streets disappeared and Gerhart was standing in the
middle of the village, the heat from the bonfire
prickling his face.

It was not as hot as he might have expected, for
standing around the blaze was a cordon of zealots.

Gerhart took them all in with a disapproving glance. Some wore hooded habits, whilst others wore the clothes of commoners. Some had shaved their heads, as was the way of many who joined the priesthood of Sigmar, but others had allowed their hair and beards to grow into thick, unkempt manes.

They all sported some kind of symbol or icon of the Heldenhammer. And they all had the haunted look of desperate men – men who had suffered such hardship and tragedy in their lives that they now had nothing to live for but their faith and the persecution of the sinful.

They were all armed, and one matted-hair individual was using the knotted whip he was carrying on himself. He beat his back repeatedly over first one shoulder and then the other, his unintelligible mutterings punctuated by sharp intakes of breath or impulsive gasps of pain.

'Flagellants and fanatics,' Gerhart growled. 'Madmen all.'

'Who is this sinner?' a voice, loud and clear as a cannon shot, demanded over the crackling of the bonfire.

Gerhart turned to see a dishevelled, rag-robed figure pointing at him. The flesh of the man's outstretched arm was scabrous and coloured a sickly green-grey. He had obviously once been dressed the same way as the other flagellants, in a tunic embroidered with the golden twin-tailed comet of Sigmar, but his habit was now torn and stained, looking more like a burial shroud.

The speaker was surrounded by four hulking figures that, although dressed like holy men, had the build and stance of bodyguards.

Despite being a whole head shorter than the hulking Sigmarites surrounding him, the man had an air
of authority that distinguished him as their leader.

Close to the man, Gerhart gagged on the sickly
sweet smell of decay. Was this because he was at the
heart of another damned settlement that had fallen
prey to the plague or was the smell coming from the
bandage-bound figure in front of him, he wondered?

The wizard could not see the man's face. Under
the pulled up hood of the habit the zealots' leader
wore a shaped leather mask, stained almost black,
which gave him a leering, almost daemonic, expression. Stuffed into a cracked leather belt at his waist
was a scourging whip, its several knotted lengths of
leather embedded with cruel barbs and spikes.

The wizard did not bother to hide his revulsion.

When the leader of the zealots spoke again, Gerhart was certain that the gagging stench was
emanating from the diseased man.

'I say again, what sinner is this who would interrupt our holy work? Why has he not been judged?
Seize him!'

'I too could ask who you are,' Gerhart retaliated.
'What are you doing here, and what are you doing
to these people?'

Suddenly Gerhart found him surrounded by half a
dozen Sigmarite zealots, some of them abandoning
their position at the fire, others emerging out of the
coiling ash-flecked smoke.

He brought his staff up before him in both hands
but the fanatics were on him, batting aside the
wizard's oaken rod with swipes of iron-banded
maces. Gerhart received two sharp blows from the

haft-end of a pole arm. Something blunt and heavy smacked into his ribs from behind. Startled, and gasping for breath, he felt rough hands grab him.

Gerhart could feel Aqshy's energies surging into him, drawn at first by the bonfires, visible to his mage-sight as coruscating ribbons of scarlet energy and fluctuating crimson light. But it was a source of power that he was unable to tap, his arms were being held firmly at his sides, and his staff had been wrested from his grip by one of the zealot thugs. Another man scrabbled at Gerhart's scabbarded sword and, after some struggling, managed to pull it free.

Without his weapons and so his powers of sorcery, Gerhart had nothing left but his temper.

'Do you not know who I am?'

'Why, should I?' the leader sneered.

'I am a renowned wizard of the Bright college of magic in Altdorf!' Gerhart declared, pulling himself up to his full height.

'Ah, so you are one of those who would bring ruin to our great nation by consorting with the powers of darkness!' It was not a question; the man had already made his judgement. 'All those who play with fire end up getting burned,' he said, half-turning to the raging bonfire behind him.

What was the man talking about, Gerhart asked himself? He was talking and behaving like a fanatica follower of Sigmar, but his physical appearance was enough to make any rational man suspect the monk was not all he proclaimed to be.

How could the man be so unaware of his own condition, unless it was not only his body that had been corrupted but his mind as well?

'Curse you for a damned fool!' Gerhart growled. 'Do you believe you are doing Sigmar's work here?'

'Have you not seen the signs?' the leader wailed. 'The End Times are upon us! The servants of Chaos are at large in the world and if the light of Sigmar's truth is to shine through the darkness we must light the way with the burning bodies of his enemies!'

Gerhart considered the evil signs he had already seen abroad in the land, the two-headed foal at the isolated farm in Stosten, the still-born spider-legged baby in Avenhoff, the rain of fish in Vlatch, the leering green-tinged face of the second moon as it traversed the sky, and now the sickness afflicting the very Sigmarite zealots who would rid Ostland of the plague.

Maybe this truly was the beginning of the prophesied End Times?

A sharply raised eyebrow was the only indication Gerhart made that he considered there to be anything amiss, the rest of his face an inscrutable mask.

There was a definite miasma of disease and decay in the air. A zealot shoved a moaning villager past him. Although Gerhart was no physician, the so-called plague victim appeared to have little obviously wrong with him. The warrior priest wondered if the same held true for the other people the zealots were rounding up and throwing into the flames of the growing funeral pyre?

By contrast to the villagers, these fanatical Sigmarites had definitely contracted the disease at some stage, possibly whilst carrying out their holy work. Fat, hairy bluebottles buzzed around the holy men, whose skin was blistered with buboes and weeping ulcers. Their faces – those that he could see

– were drawn and gaunt, with great coal rings around sunken, red-rimmed eyes. And these signs of sickness were no greater than around the rag-shrouded, flagellant monk himself.

Outnumbered and alone, Gerhart knew that he had to save himself and get out of this village before he too became caught up in this madness. And he had to do so now.

'You have been in contact with the diseased. Could it be that you too have succumbed to this vile sickness?' Gerhart challenged the monk.

'No!' the leader yelled, clearly unaware of his own corrupted condition. 'We are carrying out holy work, the sacred mission given to us by Sigmar himself in a vision of glory.'

'And what is that mission?'

'Can you not see?' the Sigmarites' leader said, indicating a huddle of terrified villagers being held by yet more of his sinister followers. 'These creatures are the servants of Nurgle!' Gerhart felt his stomach lurch at hearing the plague god's true name. 'They bear the stigmata of the Lord of Decay's chosen ones. While they live to spread their master's filth and corruption, the carrion lord grows fat and bloated on the souls of the innocent and his dark power swells in the world, like a cadaver swelling with corpse gases.'

Gerhart couldn't believe what he was hearing. Everything he had seen in Grunhafen suggested that it was the villagers who were the innocent ones and the Sigmarite host, blind to the truth, who had been corrupted by the Lord of Decay.

Look at them, thought the wizard. Look how unhealthy they all are!

As if to affirm Gerhart's observations, one of the zealots broke into a hacking cough.

'How dare you make such accusations? Enough of this! It is you who are the evil ones! And it is you who must be judged!'

At that, Gerhart stamped down hard on the foot of one of the zealots holding him. In shock and pain the man let go of him and took a limping hop backwards. With one arm free, Gerhart took a swing at the second of his captors. His fist punched into the brute's sternum causing the man to stagger back winded. Gerhart pulled himself free of the man's weakened grip and snatched his staff back.

In two bounds Gerhart was on the leader. Even though the thought of getting closer to the diseased zealot filled him with revulsion it had to be done. Desperate times made men do desperate things.

As the monk raised his ulcerated hands to fend off the wizard, Gerhart swung his staff upwards, skilfully connecting with the man's leather mask and knocking it from his face.

As the Sigmarites closed on Gerhart to defend their master again he shouted, 'Look at your leader! Look at what he truly is!'

So full of authority was the wizard's voice that the closest zealots turned their eyes upon the ruin of their leader's face. The man's cheeks and forehead were ravaged and hollow with pockmarks. He had no nose left, just a gaping hole in the front of his face through which rotting bone and cartilage could be seen. His lips were fleshless and drawn, and as the leper screamed, Gerhart saw that the man's gums were bleeding and pulled back from brown, cracked teeth. On the man's right temple, three large, weeping buboes, were clumped together, green-yellow pus oozing from them and crusting on his veiny skin.

Gerhart could hear no gasps of revulsion or horror from the fanatics. Surely such a sight would drive zealots to either slay their master or abandon him as their leader?

'Are you all mad? Look at your master!' the wizard exclaimed again.

Still no one moved.

Still screaming hysterically, the leper was scrabbling in the dirt to recover his mask.

Gerhart was amazed. In spite of everything, part of the leper's ruined mind must have realised that his appearance was abhorrent and had to be hidden from view. But still his devoted followers could not see the corruption before their very eyes.

Gerhart was suddenly aware that the buzzing of the flies had increased in intensity, as if the insects had become enraged. Then they were swarming at him in a great black cloud.

Picturing the flame burning within his mind and observing the flow of magic around the blazing pyre with his wizard-sight, Gerhart reached out with his mind and pulled a snaking tendril of orange-red energy from the air.

A cone of fire burst from the outstretched fingertips of his right hand as he thrust it towards the furious swarm. The roar of the flames drowned the buzzing of the flies as Gerhart's spell immolated their tiny black bodies.

Then the plague-bearing doom-mongers ran at him, armed with all manner of weapons, from pitchforks and worn blades to pole-arms and even the whips they used to mortify their own flesh.

Gerhart's hands began to make signs of conjuration as if he could draw on the hot, dry wind of Aqshy into himself. Surrounded by the fires of Grunhafen, and suffused with the power of the four primal elements, Gerhart could barely contain the energies welling up inside him like magma bubbling up within the heart of a volcano.

This was nothing like the struggle he had faced atop the Tower of Heaven, battling the astromancer Kozma Himmlisch. Now the spells came easily to him, with little need to truly focus his mind. He raised his hands once more and thrust them towards the approaching circle of zealots.

He had been on the verge of losing his temper and now that he was freed of their clutches he was able to release his pent-up rage in an eruption of flame. The spell burst from his hands with an animalistic roar. It was as if the flames were alive, raging and hungry like some feral beast.

Half a dozen Sigmarites fell back screaming as their heavy robes caught fire. Two of the men who had managed to retain their senses flung themselves to the ground and rolled over and over to put out the flames. Gerhart was aware of a wild-haired flagellant smacking at flames in his beard with burning hands; his high-pitched screams cut through the air in an agonised wail.

Gerhart turned his furious gaze on the man still holding his sword. To the terrified Sigmarite it seemed that the wizard's eyes were aflame. Gerhart didn't need to give the man another demonstration of his power. The zealot cast the sword before him, turned tail and fled.

Armed with his sword, staff and spells, Gerhart could now launch himself fully against the plague-corrupted zealots. But the wizard was still aware of the huge numbers of fanatics he had to face alone. He would never be able to defeat them all, he had to decide whether to make a stand or try to escape.

And then, as if in answer to an unspoken prayer, he heard pounding hooves and gruff shouts from the other side of the village square. Keeping the fanatics closest to him at bay with another blast of fiery magic, Gerhart looked through the white hot flames to see six black-clad figures riding into the thick of the diseased Sigmarites and cutting them down with bloodied swords.

Chaos and confusion reigned. The leper was screaming orders to his devotees exhorting them to kill those who would stop them from completing their holy work. Villagers ran screaming from their captors as the Sigmarites fought back against the new arrivals. Some braver individuals tried to cut down the wizard.

It was clear who the leader of the warband was: a man, tall in the saddle, wearing a high broad-brimmed black hat and holding a silver flintlock pistol. Gerhart had encountered his like before.

The man rode towards him, taking aim. For a moment doubt flickered through Gerhart's mind and the flame in his mind's eye sputtered. He clearly heard the report of the pistol firing and saw the puff of blue smoke wreath its muzzle. A split second later he heard a choked cry behind him. He turned to see a Sigmarite, chain-flail above his head, fall backwards into the fire, with a ragged red hole in his throat.

Gerhart felt he should offer some words of thanks when he heard the horseman say, 'Caught in the act.'

Before he could turn again something heavy connected with the back of his head and Gerhart's world exploded into darkness.

BEFORE THE SORCERER could slump unconscious from the coshing he had been dealt by the butt of his pistol, Gottfried Verdammen slung an arm under his shoulders and pulled him up onto the back of his panting steed. The horse barely slowed as he did so.

Having recovered after the warband's surprise attack, the crazed zealots were now running at the witch hunter and his henchmen, slashing at their steeds as well as the riders. Verdammen's men rained hacking blows down on the plague monks in an attempt to keep them at bay.

'We are done here!' Verdammen shouted to his party. 'We have what we came for. Ride on!'

Kicking his heels into his mount's flanks, Verdammen urged his stallion forward. As he did so the animal reared up and crushed the bald, blistered head of a Sigmarite heretic under its iron-shod hooves.

As he moved off to freedom and safety, with his prisoner slung across the back of his horse, Verdammen heard a sickening roar – the sound of something large, angry and hungry.

The horrific noise was soon joined by the appalled cries of those who had been left behind. Verdammen didn't know what was happening and didn't intend to find out. With another shout of encouragement to his steed he galloped out of the doomed village, with his warband, leaving the people of Grunhafen and their insane accusers to their fate. He had business elsewhere.

FOUR
The Raven's Feast

'Famine is the embodiment of the ecstasy the servants of the Prince of Chaos seek when all other sensation has lost any meaning for them. It is extreme, perverse, unhealthy, and can only end in death.'

– From the sermons of Saint Hildegard
the Chaste

By LATE SPRING of the year 2521 the news of an impending invasion from the north had been building for some time. At first it had been mere rumour and superstition, brought about by the strange omens and dire portents that had beset the land, such as the appearance of the fiery twin-tailed comet in the skies above the Empire. The reactions of those who led and protected the people of the mighty realm were mixed and contradictory.

71

Many who feared the political, social or mercantile instability that rumours alone might bring discounted the rumours as doom-mongering of heretics who would see the Empire fall. Suspected agitators were rounded up, put to trial and executed. In the wool town of Feuerpfahl alone one hundred and thirteen panic-spreaders were brought before the courts and burnt at the stake in a series of mass executions. It was said that the air around Feuerpfahl smelt of burning fat for weeks afterwards.

Others reacted to the stories that the End Times were almost upon them by cutting themselves off from the rest of the world, either in the vain hope that they might escape the impending disaster or to simply face the end, when it came, in seclusion, with their loved ones.

Others saw it as their role to take the fight to the enemy before the enemy came to them. Musters of free companies occurred throughout the Empire, from Ostermark to as far south as Wissenland. Men who had once fought in the standing armies of the elector counts quit the homes they had bought with their army pensions and reported for duty once more. Villages and towns prepared to defend themselves. Great sprawling cavalcades of fanatical holy men and their zealous followers wandered the land, doing what they saw as Sigmar's work.

The cathedrals, temples and shrines of Sigmar had never seen their congregations so numerous, or their collection plates so full. And yet it seemed that there had never been so many cults and heretics publicly turning their back on the faith of Sigmar. Idolaters went so far as to ransack a church in Turmstadt and raze it to the ground.

Bands of babbling heretics roamed the land in hordes, attacking the faithful even while at prayer. They carried out their own blasphemous trials of prominent religious figures, who they accused of failing the common people, lining their own pockets whilst the common folk starved, hiding in cathedral-strongholds whilst the people faced the predations of darker things. Beastmen, cultists and even the vile skaven emerged from the bowels of the earth to feast on the dying carcass of the Empire.

People spoke of the rise of the ratmen, the spread of plague and the increase in monstrous, deformed births as signs that the End Time was upon them. Omens had been scryed by soothsayers, sorcerers and village wise-women in crystal balls, and in the patterns described by the stars, as well as the mutations of the afflicted. How could anyone doubt it?

Some said the regular forays of beastmen herds from the forests of the Drakwald and the Forest of Shadows proved that the power of Chaos was on the increase. Others said that the raids were nothing unusual and simply proved that life was continuing as normal.

Scholars who had read of such things in the secret histories of the Imperial archives said the Empire was in the same state it had been before the destruction of Mordheim, that depraved city of the damned, or before the last great Chaos incursion over three hundred years before, which had been repelled by Magnus the Pious.

Some began decrying the state of the nation, saying that there were no more heroes like those of old. Those who were braver, or more foolish, than the rest went so far as to accuse the Emperor Karl-Franz himself of not doing enough to halt the advance of Chaos. The people began to look for new heroes to save them, and in the Reikland rumour said that such a hero had been found.

With the initial incursions into the frozen land of Kislev by the marauder hordes of the north, what many had suspected for a long time could no longer be denied. The sense of doom and panic pervading the Empire, already bad, grew worse.

Yet this was also a time of great optimism. Differences between rival noblemen were put aside, personal aggrandisement were forgotten by some political leaders, and the needs of the many were put before the needs of the few. Temples emptied their coffers to aid the preparations for the battles to come.

It was a time of contradictions; a time of Chaos.

As news continued to stream in from Kislev and the north-eastern edge of the Empire, the official call to arms went out and the muster of troops began in earnest. Every province and city-state prepared to defend itself against attack by the daemonic armies of the north.

Far to the north of the Empire, in the shadow of the Middle Mountains, the sentinel city of Wolfenburg, domain of Elector Count Valmir von Raukov, also made ready. As his standing army prepared to hold back the tide of evil that scouts declared was heading their way, word reached Valmir that troops were coming to the aid of his city. Whether out of some noble sense of duty or an attempt to stem the tide of Chaos sweeping south, it mattered not. What mattered was that help was on its way.

The city of Wolfenburg was far from a defenceless target. Its ancient walls had held back countless

sieges in the past, and its standing army was proud
and strong. It had often led the offensive against the
enemy into the querulous borderlands or mountain
reaches where renegades and rebels gathered, along
with bandits and other inhuman enemies. The city's
forces were combined with a number of Templar
orders who saw it as their holy duty to protect this
edge-of-the-Empire bastion and safeguard the security of the rest of the nation that lay beyond the
wilds of Ostland.

The stern-faced elector count expressed relief
when he heard that a cannon train had been dispatched from the smelting works of Schmiedorf to
bolster the defences of the sentinel city.

While the guards watched and Wolfenburg waited,
reports of the Chaos hordes' steady encroachment
into the lands of mortal men continued. Doom-
mongers were heard to whisper a name that froze
the hearts of men. Mention of it made men make
the sign of the hammer, touch iron or bless themselves.

And the name was Archaon, dread lord of the End
Times himself.

This was a Chaos incursion unparalleled in the
history of the Empire and Sigmar's people were crip-
pled by their fear.

As they sharpened their sword blades in the
armouries, or tended to their steeds in the stables,
certain Templar knights heard the name, the
rumours, and the terror in the voices that spoke it.
They resolved then that it was time to honour the
holy vows they had made.

* * *

ON THE TWELFTH day of Pflugzeit dawn broke cold
and brittle. Despite the unseasonable chill, the
severe weather that had plagued Ostland for the last
month seemed to have passed, for that morning the
sun rose, no longer cloaked by cloud.

An hour after dawn, the hazy yellow-white disc of
the sun travelled a path across the firmament and
mist began rising from the meadows outside the city
walls. The great gates of Wolfenburg were heaved
open to emit a host of knights who rode out from
between the gate towers.

The thunder of their horses' hooves resounded as
twenty riders, two abreast, their captain and standard bearer ahead of the charge, emerged from the
city. They were knights of the Templar order of Sigmar's Blood.

They were truly a sight to behold: lustrous helms,
glittering vambraces and cuirasses flashed silver in
the morning light; lances were raised high, and a
forest of spear tips gleamed in the sun's rays. The
horses' hooves beat a tattoo of war on the ground.
Pennants and banners of white cloth embroidered
with red and gold flapped above the riders' heads.

One standard carried at the head of the armoured
force was greater and more impressive than all the
others. Its cloth was aged and threadbare, the
colours of the silks on the crest faded and worn. The
metal mountings of the dark-stained banner pole
were tarnished with the patina of age and dented
out of shape. Compared to the other flags and pennants carried by the host, it was dull, dark and
dusty, a relic of another age.

It was a standard that had seen war; that had been
carried into battle at the head of many a victorious

army. This standard had never been captured, and had always returned to its venerated resting place in the chapel of Sigmar at the Elector Count of Ostland's castle seat. The mere presence of the standard filled the knights with a resolve as strong as steel. They would complete their task and conquer any foe they met on their mission.

The knights of Sigmar's Blood were riding to meet up with an artillery train that was journeying to Wolfenburg from Schmiedorf, bringing cannon to help defend the city from attack. The knights would ensure that nothing befell those who came to the sentinel city's aid and would do their best to protect the precious artillery.

Captain Jurgen Enrich glanced over his shoulder at his Templar host. His horse panted beneath his armoured weight, and the knight could feel its powerful muscles heaving under his saddle. His heart swelled with pride at the sight of the host cantering in lines behind him. They moved as one, so well practiced were they. In times of discord and disorder, the sight of twenty of the most adept and devoted of knights would fill any honest folk with hope that the gathering storm of Chaos could be overcome.

Each one of the Templar warriors was a formidable force in his own right. Skilled with the lance, sword, axe and hammer, any one of the knights of Sigmar's Blood could face and fell a dozen attackers.

Mounted on their mighty warhorses, they were even more deadly foes. It would take a powerful opponent to best one of these knights in battle. As far as Captain Jurgen Enrich was concerned, such a thing would never happen. The paladin knights would return, with the cannon train, to be greeted by jubilant cheers from the townsfolk of Wolfenburg. They would drive the hosts of the enemy from their land, back to the barren Northern Wastes, routed and broken into pitiful warbands. The knights would bury their blades in the bodies of the degenerate followers of the lord of the End Times and make a raven's feast of his armies.

Enrich kicked his spurs into his steed's flanks and spurred the horse into a gallop. The rest of the armoured host followed suit, maintaining an orderly distance, and never breaking their formation. Clods of turf flew from the horses' hooves as they careered down the incline of the hill away from the ancient city.

As they turned into a spur of woodland, the knights disappeared beneath the trees, out of sight of the guards at the city gate. One last pennant briefly fluttered in the wind, with its tip glinting in the morning light, and then that too was gone.

THE FIRST THING that Lector Wilhelm Faustus noticed about the place, after he got through the clouds of smoke, was the stench of disease and decay in the air. The second thing was the unnatural stillness: the only sounds he could hear, other than those made by his own small entourage – the jangling of harness, the scuffing of boots on the ground, and the scrape of weapons being unsheathed – was the crackling of dying embers and the soft moan of the wind that blew flurries of dirty ash into their faces in irritating gusts. The men had followed him after the 'miracle' he had performed back in Steinbrucke.

Grunhafen, the sign read. So that was the name of the place.

The village was still partially surrounded by a stockade of sharpened tree-trunk posts, torn down in places. It had not take long for the warrior priest's party to discover why. A series of bonfires had been built up around the outskirts of the settlement.

Grunhafen seemed to have suffered the same fate as the other settlements they had passed through. At first Wilhelm thought the fires had been lit to purify the air of the contagion that had afflicted this region.

But something else had happened to this apparently once-prosperous village. Not just fires had been burning. What had happened here, and where were the people of Grunhafen?

Then the priest saw the first of the bodies.

It was the body of a man, face down on the road in front of them as they advanced warily towards the heart of the village. It was revealed as a coil of smoke was blown clear by the uneasy air. The man was wearing a monk-like habit of heavy sackcloth.

The warrior priest's entourage hung back, not as comfortable around dead bodies as the lector. Wilhelm approached the prone figure, half-consciously making the sign of the hammer over his heart.

Putting his strong calloused hand on the man's shoulder the lector turned him over. The dead eyes had rolled into the top of the man's head, and his face was disfigured by disease. The front of his robe, which was blood-stained and filthy, bore an embroidered twin-tailed comet. The man's midriff had been split by a massive wound, the purple-grey coils of his intestines spilling out.

The stench was horrendous and Wilhelm was forced to put a hand over his nose and mouth. Behind him he heard one of his entourage retch and lose his breakfast.

'What in Sigmar's name happened here?' one of his men asked, his voice weak and wavering.

'By all that's holy, I intend to find out,' Wilhelm growled, standing up again. 'Come on, this way,' he instructed, looking back at the motley collection of men who now followed him.

And with that the party continued into Grun-hafen.

As the warrior priest stepped over the corpses lit-tering the streets, including women and children, he tried not to dwell on the carnage but recalled instead how his latest entourage had come to join him.

It had been after that fateful night in Steinbrucke when he had battled the undead. The odds would have appeared insurmountable to a man without Wilhelm's faith, but for this warrior priest of Sigmar, the outcome had never been in doubt. By dawn the revenants had been returned to the grave, the uneasy souls sent on to their eternal rest. He had broken the dark path of the necromantics.

Before leaving the village, Wilhelm had set to work restoring the neglected chapel to a holy shrine once more. As he worked in the chapel, righting pews and sweeping leaves from the chalky flag-stones, the first of the penitents had come to him, full of trepidation and remorse, and seeking absolu-tion.

The lector pointed out that absolution had to be earned through acts of repentance. While some had drifted back to their godless homes, others had sworn to fight at Wilhelm's side, in the name of Sigmar, until the slate of their sins had been wiped clean.

Wilhelm stepped out from between the skeletal shells of two charred buildings into the centre of the village. 'Sigmar's hammer!' he gasped, hefting his great warhammer in his gauntleted hands, ready to fight.

There was not much that could provoke such a response from the warrior priest, what he had seen had shaken him to the core. Wilhelm took a deep breath and uttered the prayer of the humble penitent. In a moment his steely resolve returned and his face became a mask of grim determination.

Before him stood the remains of a huge bonfire, some twelve feet across. Amidst the ash and embers Wilhelm could quite clearly see the partially burnt and blackened bones and skulls of human beings. Lying around the village square, at the edge of the white circle, there were more bodies, villagers and robed figures. Sharp-beaked ravens and other dark birds probed the soft bodies for the choicest scraps.

What horrified Wilhelm most was that he could see symbols of the Sigmarite brotherhood: twin-tailed comets, smiting hammers, and the sharply angled 'S' of Sigmar amidst this carnage. It was clear that his own order had been dealt a terrible wrong.

Wilhelm felt anger rising inside him, the zealous wrath of the righteous. He heard his men muttering and shuffling a few steps backwards. The head of his warhammer was suddenly aglow with lambent flame.

He gave a shout and the ragged carrion birds rose into the air, their harsh cawing echoing through the remaining buildings around the village square.

Wilhelm closed both his eyes – the seeing one and the blind – and breathed deeply, intoning Saint Asmodius's prayer of protection as he did so. He opened his eyes and gazed upon the ruins of the village with his one good eye. He saw the smoking fires and the charred corpses but now the scene was awash with something beyond normal sight. It was as if there were colours he could smell, scents he could hear, sounds he could taste, flavours he could touch and vibrations he could see.

The priest was sensitive to powers that moved through and alongside the earthly plane. His awareness came from his focus on the godly power of Sigmar that worked through men's souls. He had sensed the… the wrongness – it was the only way he could think of it – in these currents. It was as if dark energies were being drawn to this place, in much the same way as a whirlpool would draw in the waters of the deep.

The lector began to pace around the funeral pyre. What crime could these people have possibly committed to deserve such a terrible fate? Or were they simply the victims of a plague that no one had the power to cure?

Smoke continued to rise from the smouldering embers. The latent heat distorted the air above it into a shimmering haze as though it were a summer's day.

The crows continued to harry the priest's entourage with their cawing. The charcoal skeletons of kindling crunched under Wilhelm's boots and the wind moaned softly. Then the priest became aware of another sound. He paused.

It was the sound of something living, but it was so horrid it would have turned a weaker man's stomach. It was the sound of feasting, the tearing of flesh and the cracking of bones.

The ghastly sound was coming from the burnt-out remains of a fire-ravaged house. At first Wilhelm could not make sense of what he was seeing through the blackened beams and half-tumbled walls of the building, so malformed was its grotesquely overgrown body. Then the creature shifted its obscene bulk with a wallowing *whoomph* and great gust of expelled air.

His followers, trailing along behind him, had seen the thing too.

'Sigmar's bones!' cried one. Another began to pray with the urgency of a penitent on his deathbed. Wilhelm could also hear weeping.

The abomination had heard them too.

Raising its great, eyeless head, the beast swung it in their direction, as if it were looking straight at them. Ropes of human entrails swung slackly from jaws that were oddly placed on its body.

Wilhelm heard someone behind him vomit again.

The abomination was of a monstrous size, fully as long as the ruins of the house it now wallowed in and the hump of its body was almost as tall as a man. The bulk of the creature's huge, distorted body resembled an enormous segmented slug. Its wet, grey flesh rippled obscenely every time it moved. Protruding rather incongruously from its body were spindly multi-jointed limbs, ending in single hooked claws or writhing rubbery tentacles.

Despite its slug-like form, the vertebrae of a malformed spine could be seen through the taut grey flesh of the monster's back. Along this ridge, thickened bony plates afforded the creature some protection whilst the hooked talons, writhing tentacles and pseudo-pods could help the creature defend itself.

The creature showed signs of sickness, the surface of its disgusting skin was covered with patches of huge, blistering boils that popped and oozed their filth regularly.

Having surveyed the horror-struck warband, the creature flopped back down amidst the ruins and continued to consume its meal of half-burnt, rotting corpses in the shell of the fire ravaged house.

Wilhelm knew what they were facing. He had seen such a thing once before, when he had been fighting on a battlefield under a bloody sky against the degenerate followers of the Fell Powers. He recognised it too from nightmares that came to him unbidden during the darkest watches of the night.

It was a freakish parody of a living thing. It had quite possibly once been human, but it was no longer. It was a mindless thing, a spawn of Chaos, its only motivation being to feed on the rotting corpses of the dead, and to kill. Judging by its size, it must have consumed a fair amount of flesh.

'Men of Sigmar!' Wilhelm declared, taking a step forward. 'Such an abomination cannot be allowed to live! In the name of the Heldenhammer, attack!'

Yelling like a maniac, the warrior priest charged towards the ruined house and the spawn lurking within it, raising his glowing warhammer above his head. Hurdling a broken section of wall, Wilhelm crashed into the blackened rubble and landed a mighty blow on the abomination's head with his blessed weapon.

The pallid flesh rippled under the blow and the creature jerked back instinctively. A horrible mewling whine escaped its jaws as it tried to retract its head inside its body.

A bony claw lashed out at him, but Wilhelm was too quick. With his muscles straining, he brought the warhammer round again and hit the spindly, crab-like limb with a resounding crack, snapping it backwards. The creature whined again.

His small entourage joined the battle, fighting with the zeal of the converted, raining blows down upon the abomination. However, it was obvious that these men were not trained fighters. They had been common labouring folk, farmers, millers, shepherds and the like, drawn to his cause by the valour and faith he had shown in battle. One of them, a grey-haired man by the name of Kuhlbert, had fought as a halberdier in the army of Ostland twenty years ago, but age was getting the better of him now.

With little in the way of actual swordsmanship, Wilhelm's accomplices did not strike effectively at the spawn's vulnerable points with their blades. Their blows were turned aside by rubbery tentacles and armoured scales. So whilst the others did little more than irritate the spawn, it was up to the warrior priest to destroy it.

Wilhelm swung his hammer round in an arc from the right. The solid iron head connected with the monster's jaw, splintering teeth from its mouth and sending a spray of filthy blood into the air.

Emitting a guttural, throaty bellow from the depths of its chest, the abomination rose up on its muscular tail. Strings of slime oozed from its underbelly that elastically touched the ground. Its broad head towered some twelve feet above the ground.

Wilhelm noticed the most horrific thing about the monstrosity. In the middle of the creature's thorax were horribly stretched and distorted features of a human face. The priest was sure he could hear a weak mewling noise coming from the quivering lips of the face, and thought he saw tears running from the slits of its eyes through the slime. But no matter how human and pitiful the face appeared, the spawn was nothing more than a mindless beast.

The creature threw its whole body forward to crush its attacker. Wilhelm leapt out of the way but the less experienced man behind him, confused by the chaos of the battle, was not quick enough.

The spawn crashed down on top of the man, covering him entirely. The horrific creature pulled its tail forward, sliding on its slime-trail through the rubble and then rose up on its strong tail again to repeat the manoeuvre. Wilhelm staggered backwards, trying to maintain his balance and stop himself being killed.

As the beast rose up the crushed man was revealed. He was struggling weakly, and gagging on the sticky filth that clogged his mouth. The monster flopped down again, sending clouds of ash billowing into the air. The attackers coughed.

Up close, Wilhelm was aware of the putrescent stench put out by the creature: an acrid mix of bile, the ammonia stink of sewage and the sickly-sweet reek of rotting meat. The spawn opened its maw and

Wilhelm could quite clearly see the rows of shark-like teeth receding into the dark hole of its gullet.

Aware of a movement out of the corner of his eye he swung round, instinctively bringing his warhammer up to parry any incoming attack. The creature had struck at him with a mottle-fleshed limb that extended elastically from the side of its loathsome body. Snapping at the end of this pod-tentacle was another fang-lined mouth, large enough to take a man's head off. The tentacle struck again like a swaying cobra.

Wilhelm smacked the head of his hammer into the mouth and with a twist of his wrist caught it and flung it onto the ground. The initial impact tore the maw open along one side. The head was stuccoed with gobbets of meat, and the mouth twitched spasmodically. Wilhelm brought his hammer down again, crushing the pod-head to a messy pulp.

The warrior priest rained blow after blow down upon the spawn, rupturing its horrid flesh, bursting pus-filled boils and fracturing what bones there were inside its mollusc body. The monster responded by whipping at him with its tentacles, snapping at him with its horribly distended jaws and clawing at him with its ungainly, multi-jointed, taloned limbs. They scraped against the iron of his breastplate, and sliced through the heavy cloth of his robes, drawing blood from his flesh with its claws. He was coated in the filth and slime discharged by the spawn, and its dark blood stained his cowled cloak.

His relentless blows seemed to be having little effect; the beast's grotesque bulk absorbed the damage. He did nothing other than drive the creature into an animal rage, which showed no signs of abating.

Wilhelm could feel his muscles beginning to tire. He needed to try a different approach. It would take more than weapons to destroy this monster.

If he could stir one of the bonfires back into life he was certain the flames would prove an effective weapon. But in the time it would take him to achieve such a thing the abomination might well have put an end to him and those who now fought at his side. To simply turn and flee would be neglecting his duty and would be a blasphemy against Sigmar's will.

'Keep it busy!' he commanded his men and took a step back.

If Wilhelm was beginning to feel exhaustion creeping up on him, then that was nothing compared to what the others must be feeling. Nevertheless, his puffing and panting followers redoubled their attacks against the spawn, striking at it from all sides.

Wilhelm had to admire their fortitude, taking on a horror such as this. But then they had already seen their own fair share of horrors stalking the streets of Steinbrucke. Their attacks were having little real impact against the spawn but at least they were keeping it busy, so Wilhelm could prepare himself.

The priest closed his eyes and began to pray. Sinking into a semi-trance-like state he was only dimly aware of a cry from one of the men.

It was cut short by a sickening crunch, and was followed by terrified protests of the rest of his party. When the warrior priest opened his eyes again, they were orbs of fire.

As he drew upon the glorious light of Sigmar, and the righteous fury that such an abomination should defile the face of the world, a lambent golden glow surrounded him.

As if understanding it did not have long to live, the Chaos spawn made one last desperate lunge at the warrior priest. Wilhelm stood his ground. The creature was within three feet of him when pure white light flashed and burnt the air above him. It was as if the abomination had struck some invisible shield created by the priest's faith.

The spawn recoiled, great black weals and blisters burned into the underside of its body and covered the stretched human face. Before it could recover Wilhelm strode in, swinging the fiery head of his warhammer in a figure of eight pattern.

He struck once, twice, three times – half-congealed blood and corruption spurting from wound after wound. The spawn sank back, its spine arching backwards, and then collapsed in on itself.

Wilhelm waited, warhammer at the ready, for another sudden impulsive attack.

And waited.

No attack came.

He heard an unpleasant fizzing, gurgling sound as the hideous Chaos spawn's body turned in on itself. The pallid flesh of the slug-thing began to bubble and ripple as if worms were crawling under its skin. Its shape changed from the inside out.

Wilhelm tightened his grip on the haft of the warhammer as the creature lurched into the air once more. An agonised howl rose from the monster's jaws as the scarred human face gave a scream that turned the blood of all who heard it to ice.

The creature's sides heaved, and it started to spew out a stream of blood. Quickly it became clear to the horrified observers that the creature was regurgitating its own organs, effectively turning itself inside out. Muscles and thick cords of intestines twitched and spasmed, and the lector could see new bony limbs forming within the mass, straining at the contorting, bubbling flesh as they did so.

Wilhelm could sense the waves of energy writhing around the monster, to fuel its metamorphosis.

The Chaos spawn spasmed one last time and from somewhere within the bloody offal-flesh there came a rattling, gargling cry that could be nothing other than a death-howl.

The convulsions stopped and the pile of flesh sagged, then dissolved. There could be no doubt that the abomination was dead at last.

'Where now, your holiness?' Kuhlbert asked, as they prepared to leave the destroyed village. They had lost two of their number in the fight against the Chaos spawn.

Climbing into Kreuz's saddle, the lector paused. They were gathered at the shattered remains of the north gate leading out of Grunhafen. Where there had been few signs of traffic from the south, here the tracks had been churned by the passage of men and horses. Whoever had been here, and witnessed or taken part in this carnage, had left heading in that direction.

'North,' Wilhelm stated in his deep booming voice.

'The city of Wolfenburg lies in that direction,' Kuhlbert said.

'Dark things are afoot in this land,' Wilhelm said grimly, turning his stern gaze on his followers, 'and I fear the city could be in danger. I sense a time of great evil is near, a time when we will all have our part to play.'

Turning Kreuz's head to the north, Wilhelm kicked his heels into his steed's sides and led the way out of the ruined village.

FIVE
Trial by Fire

*'The Sword of Judgement hangs
over me now, and all I see around me
is a shadowy web of secrets and lies.
Secrets and lies.'*

– Osrus Fogweaver before his execution as
a heretic by the Council of Siedlung

GERHART OPENED HIS eyes. There was no light in the
cell. Through the tiny barred arch of a window fif-
teen feet above him, all he could see were the
pinpricks of stars set into an arc of deepest blue. He
could feel the damp chill of the stone wall against
his back, leaving him numb with cold.

It felt as if the dark, dank cell had leeched the heat
from the very marrow of his bones and had taken
his strength with it. He was half-sitting in a corner

of the room. As his eyesight gradually adjusted to the gloom Gerhart began to discern objects amongst the amorphous black shapes in his vision.

In front of him, on the other side of the cell, were a few shallow stone steps that led up to a sturdy iron-banded oak door, with heavy hinges and a small barred grille at head height. The steps were wet with slime and smooth from years of use.

There was nothing more to his prison than bare stone walls, steps and a wooden door. Rusted chains and manacles dangled from the vaulted roof. Whoever maintained this cell took punishment very seriously.

He could remember little after he had been knocked senseless. There had been brief periods when he had been shaken into head-aching consciousness, only for his world to fade to fuzzy grey again moments later.

He did remember being slung onto the back of a horse and jolted into unconsciousness again as the creature galloped from the madness in the village of Grunhafen. And he'd been aware of the ride through the enclosing dark of a forest and the sound of hounds barking in the distance. He had only been half-conscious when the party arrived at this nameless village where he was now prisoner. He vaguely recalled the clattering of keys in a lock, the gruff complaints of rough, sweat-stinking men then the numbing cold of the cell.

A thought suddenly struck Gerhart and he felt for his sword belt. It was gone. So had his staff, although his captors had left him with the numerous other charms and totems he wore.

His head ached. He did not know how long he had been unconscious but thought it unlikely that it had been much more than a day, or he might not have recovered his senses at all.

As far as he could tell, he was at least partly below ground, and that was why it was damp and cold. In fact it was as icy as a cold store. Lying there, unconscious and inactive for the gods knew how long, the cold had taken a great deal of power from him.

He closed his eyes and then opened them again to his wizard-sight. He could see the icy-blue and frosty-green currents of other magical energies trailing like marsh lights through the darkness of the cell. The tendrils of power he sought were not drawn to dark, damp cold places: in fact such environments repulsed them. No flame burned in his mind's eye.

A warm, yellow-orange glow suddenly appeared beyond the bars of the grille in the cell door. Gerhart heard the rattling of keys accompanied by low, hissing voices. He could not make out what they were saying although he thought one of them sounded familiar.

With a creak of rusted hinges the cell door was heaved open and a man stepped into the cell, silhouetted by the glaring light of a lantern held by another.

In the wizard's mind's eye light sparked in the darkness.

Gerhart put a hand up to shield his eyes as the witch hunter approached him. As well as the black-clad Sigmarite and the lantern-bearer, Gerhart could see two other figures moving in the flickering light and shadows. These two followed the witch hunter into the gaol cell.

'Where am I?' Gerhart asked crossly.

The witch hunter ignored his question. 'Bind him,' he instructed.

Gerhart struggled to get to his feet as the two burly men closed on him. But in his aching weakened state the lean wizard could do little to stop these stronger men. They seized him, forcing his arms behind his back. A rope was tied around his wrists, to bind them, pulled so tight it cut into his flesh. The witch hunter's lackeys hauled Gerhart to his feet.

'Where are you taking me?' the wizard demanded.

The witch hunter looked back at him disinterestedly, but did not answer.

'Answer me!' Gerhart demanded, feeling fury building inside him.

'Take him to the chamber,' was all the witch hunter said, again speaking only to the escorts.

With a minder either side of him, Gerhart was half-marched and half-dragged from the cell.

THE CELL DOOR was opened once more and Gerhart pushed inside. He stumbled down the slick steps into the gloom and fell to his knees on the chill stone floor. The door slammed shut behind him and was locked again. Gerhart rolled onto his side, contorting in agony as he put pressure on the bruises and weals now covering his back, arms and legs.

His body was a map of pain. The sadistic witch hunter had known what he was doing. Where other, less experienced torturers would have used hot coals, heated pokers and naked flames to exact a confession, the witch hunter had instructed his torturer to use a combination of blunt instruments and icy cold water.

He winced as he rested his bruised cheek on the cold, wet stones of the cell floor. His torment had lasted for hours, the witch hunter calmly asking him the same questions over and over. He repeated the same accusations, and Gerhart strenuously denied them all.

The witch hunter's words echoed in Gerhart's mind, fresh as the agonies the blubbery, leather-hooded torturer had inflicted on him.

'Who is your master? Which of the Fell Powers have you sold your soul to?'

'When did you turn to the worship of the Dark Gods?'

'You are a devotee of Chaos, are you not?'

'What made you turn your back on the Empire and Lord Sigmar?'

'Confess! You are the lap-dog of your Chaos masters. Confess! Confess everything!'

The screams of his denials echoed alongside the accusations.

He had been able to do nothing else. He had been tied to the torturer's blood-stained table, with his hands bound, so there was no way that he could have used his magic. Anger boiled inside him, hot enough to melt metal.

But his resolve had been great and before he cracked, the witch hunter had brought the agonising proceedings to an end.

Gerhart knew what his fate would be and while it rested in the hands of the cold-hearted witch hunter, there was nothing he could do but wait. But if the witch hunter thought his prey would go quietly, he was sadly mistaken. The Sigmarite would rue the day he had earned the enmity of Gerhart Brennend.

* * *

GERHART SLEPT FITFULLY and when he awoke the grey half-light of dusk was descending beyond the tiny barred window.

Every part of his body ached, he was hungry and cold, and the rope binding his hands was chafing his skin. Barely-contained anger bubbled just beneath the surface, waiting for an opportunity to be released in a furious outburst of vengeance.

Hearing keys rattling in the lock Gerhart cautiously craned his neck to see the same orange glow outside the door as he had before.

This time the two men entered the cell without their master. Gerhart didn't speak and did not struggle as they brusquely lugged him to his feet and hauled him from the dungeon again.

Instead of taking him to the torture chamber, the two guards led him along different passageways and up through the sturdy stone-built building. He noticed that the torches held in iron brackets and stone sconces throughout the tunnels were unlit. The twilight coming through narrow arrow-slit windows was enough for them to see by.

Before he knew it, they were outside the village's gaol-cum-gatehouse and making their way through the silent streets down towards a mill. Its huge groaning waterwheel creaked as it turned in the steady flow of the stream that had been diverted to power it.

Gathered at the edge of the millpond was the entire population of the village, waiting in eager anticipation.

GERHART STUDIED THE circle of wards around him. Three concentric rings of esoteric sigils had been inscribed in the packed earth, the runes and markings picked out in coloured powders. They were quite beautiful to look at and whoever had created them knew what he was doing. Gerhart could feel the magical power throbbing from them in numbing waves. He could see the sparkling rainbow-coloured tendrils with his enhanced wizard's vision, and he could understand their purpose.

Once again he had to admit to having a grudging respect for the witch hunter. He was no mere paranoid fanatic. No, he was an educated and intelligent man who applied as much knowledge and learning to his work as he did a zeal for punishment.

Not only did the wards isolate Gerhart from the winds of magic, they also prevented him from crossing the barrier they formed. The witch hunter's men had placed him inside the wards but he knew it would not be easy to leave their confines.

Even if he could somehow break through, his bound hands would mean he could not escape. The witch hunter's men would run him through before he could get five yards. They were standing now between the villagers and the imprisoning circle.

Gerhart would have to bide his time and wait for an opportunity to present itself. While he waited, with his back to the millpond, he began to work at the knots binding his hands with long, dextrous fingers.

'You SEE BEFORE you the perpetrator of crimes against the good people of Ostland. He has the blood of innocents on his hands and has caused devastation in his rampage across the Empire,' the

witch hunter declared, addressing the crowd. He
was pointing to Gerhart as if there might be some
doubt as to who he was talking about.

'Rampage?' Gerhart interjected, unable to contain
himself any longer. 'I've never heard such balder-
dash!'

'You see at my feet the wicked tools he used on his
trail of death and destruction,' the witch hunter
said, still ignoring Gerhart. 'His fell sword and sorcerous staff.'

Cries of shock and appalled anger rose from the
crowd. Gerhart could see his sheathed sword lying
at his accuser's feet, along with the knotted rod of
his oaken staff.

The witch hunter had come to the climax of his
'trial' of the sorcerer. Frustrated anger seethed and
boiled beneath the wizard's grim-set expression.
The crowd that had been silent at his arrival were
now no better than a baying mob, hungry for blood
– his blood.

The witch hunter let the crowd express resentment
of all things sorcerous. When he felt they had had
long enough to express their dissent, he raised his
hands and spoke, his words cutting clearly through
the shouts of the crowd.

'Good people of Hochmoor, the Lord Sigmar will
look upon you with favour, in both this life and the
next, for your part in the persecution of this heretic.
I have seen the wanton destruction wrought by this
sorcerer. You may sleep peacefully this night, knowing that you have saved your own homes from
sharing the fate this murderous mage dealt Keulerdorf and Grunhafen. I, Gottfried Verdammen, witch
hunter, swear it!'

'This is ridiculous!' Gerhart shouted. 'I am a licensed wizard of the colleges of magic, renowned fire mage of the Bright order. And I will not be bound by any verdict of this mockery of a trial! You should show me respect. Do not aggravate me. I'm a dangerous man when I am angry!'

'Drown him!' a gruff voice shouted and others took up the cry.

Death by drowning. Of course, that was what the witch hunter had in mind for him. Gerhart could think of no worse an end for a fire wizard.

'This man is evil! He is a practitioner of the sorcerous arts, and he has gone too far. There is no return for him. He must be stopped. If he is allowed to live, his mere existence will encourage the growth and spread of Chaos.'

The crowd gasped.

'Prove it!' Gerhart bellowed. 'Where is your evidence? Your words are nothing but hearsay.'

Then, for the first time, Verdammen, the self-styled judge, jury and would-be executioner, addressed the wizard directly. He turned on him like a striking snake. The look in his steely eyes was cold enough to burn into Gerhart's very soul.

'So, tell me what happened in Keulerdorf!'

'That was... unfortunate,' Gerhart said, his voice suddenly quiet. He cast his eyes to the ground.

'Unfortunate?'

'You know nothing of what happened in the foothills of the Middle Mountains.'

'Why don't you tell me then?'

'What, tell you of the beast that had terrorised that village for so long? How I rid the people of their curse, and almost died? How, after all I had done for them I was hounded out of Keulerdorf by its ungrateful populace? What difference would it make? You have already decided I am guilty.'

'And how do you explain what happened to Kozma Himmlisch and the destruction of the celestial wizard's observatory-tower?'

'Will you hear my story? Listen to what I have to say?'

'He can have nothing to say that we want to hear!' a heckler cried from the crowd. 'Drown him!' Others took up the cry again.

'If you believe you have anything to say that may exonerate you, then say it. This is your chance to clear your name,' the witch hunter said over the crowd's protests.

Gerhart scowled at the man who had been so ready to believe he was a servant of Chaos and who tortured him to have his suspicions confirmed.

'I will tell my story but not so that you may judge me, but so that these good people of Hochmoor may hear it before they declare their sentence.'

The crowd jeered and bellowed in disgust, so effective was the witch hunter's rhetoric.

Verdammen calmed them with a wave of his hands. 'Go ahead then, sorcerer,' he said, fixing Gerhart with his steely gaze, and smiling coldly, 'tell your story.'

'Until his unfortunate fate befell him, I would have considered Kozma Himmlisch a friend.'

'A friend, you say?' the witch hunter interrupted. 'What about the fate that befell him?'

'Listen and I will tell you!' Gerhart snapped angrily.

'Like you, I too have noticed a rise in the power of Chaos within the land and a disruption in the flow of the winds of magic. As I said, Kozma was an old friend of mine and I thought he might be able to confirm my suspicions. I wanted to know what he had discovered in his observations of the heavens.

'When I arrived at his tower, Kozma welcomed me inside and led me up to his observatory. A huge, arcane conglomeration of brass tubes and polished crystal lenses dominated the glass-domed chamber. I noticed that the telescope was pointing to the north. I also saw a table there covered with star charts, open books and scrolls, as well as sheaves of notes Himmlisch had made. These, it turned out, concerned the appearance of the comet, as well as Kozma's observations about the flow of the currents of magical energy coming from the north.'

'How do you know this?' Verdammen asked the wizard.

'Because I took the notes from the tower and studied them later.'

A glint of delight appeared in the witch hunter's steely eyes. 'So I must add the crime of theft to your list of charges!' he said with delight, turning his smile to the gathered villagers.

'I am no thief,' Gerhart growled like a caged bear.

'But your own words condemn you!'

'Let me finish and you will see!'

The witch hunter looked back at the wizard and indicated that he should continue.

'As I was saying,' Gerhart went on, 'Kozma's magnificent telescope had been angled to the north. This was the reason for his uncharacteristic behaviour.'

'What "uncharacteristic" behaviour?' the witch hunter interjected again.

'If you did not keep interrupting me, I will get to that part of the story,' Gerhart fumed, becoming more and more troubled by the witch hunter's continual butting in.

'The longer I spent in Kozma's company, the more unsettled I became by his peculiar behaviour. He seemed agitated and kept talking to himself, and muttering unintelligibly under his breath. While Kozma was distractedly shuffling through the charts on his desk I snatched a glance through the eyepiece. I was horrified to see the leering face of the Chaos moon Morrslieb and I looked away immediately.'

There were anxious murmurs in the crowd when he mentioned the Chaos moon and many people crossed themselves with the sign of the hammer. It was clear that these simple-minded peasants did not fully understand the details of his story. They were merely cowering in fear and horror at the evil-laden words.

Verdammen, however, did nothing to interrupt Gerhart this time. The wizard must have piqued the witch hunter's interest for he seemed happy to allow him to continue with his story.

'As he chattered on, Kozma started to talk about a time of great change coming to the Empire, but he avoided the questions I put to him. Instead he just kept ranting on like some insane prophet of the End Times!'

The crowd gasped again and some began to shuffle back from the proceedings, as if Gerhart's story would damn them.

Gerhart was relieved to be able to finally relate his version of events.

'I detected a connection between Kozma's unsettled behaviour and the incessant rain outside. The heavier the downpour, the more deranged he became. Eventually the severity of the weather increased until it gave way to a sky-splitting thunderstorm.'

The witch hunter could hold his tongue no longer. 'You would accuse a member of an Imperial kommission of being deranged?' he hissed under his breath.

'An Imperial kommission? That makes no difference. He was like a man possessed!'

More gasps from the crowd.

'Then my old friend lost what reason he still had, and began howling about a rising storm of Chaos that would engulf the Old World. Then he attacked me.'

'He attacked you?' the witch hunter uttered in disbelief.

'That is what I said,' Gerhart railed.

'Then you are a liar, as well as a thief and a murderer!' Verdammen challenged.

'What? This is preposterous!'

'How could a fire wizard overcome a sorcerer of the Celestial order in the middle of a thunderstorm? I know something of the ways of spell-casters. Tempests and thunderstorms are anathema to a fire mage such as yourself, whereas they are the very source of an astromancer's power.'

'Everything I have told you is the truth!' Gerhart exploded, his rage consuming him.

The people thronging the banks of the millpond gasped and shuffled further back. Even Verdammen's men seemed somewhat perturbed to see such an outburst of furious anger. The only person who seemed unconcerned was the witch hunter.

'It is just as I suspected,' Verdammen said calmly.

'What is just as you suspected?' Gerhart fumed.

'You have gone too far with your magic. You have been corrupted by the very power that you seek to control. Chaos has your soul.' Verdammen went on. 'Wasn't it some Tilean statesman who said that all power corrupts and absolute power corrupts absolutely? Isn't that what your powers give you over us mere mortals? Absolute power?'

'What? That's nonsense!'

'Then answer me this: Chaos is the root of all magic, is it not? The mystic winds that blow from the broken gate of heaven at the heart of the Chaos-corrupted Northern Wastes provide you with power to create your spells.'

An anxious, heavy silence descended over the mob with these words. They were eager to hear how the wizard would answer.

Gerhart, his face red with anger, a vein pulsing on his forehead, took a long, deep breath. He held it for a moment, and then let it out again in a rasping huff.

'The winds of magic do indeed blow from the north but what I employ in my art is not the raw stuff of Chaos,' he explained, keeping his voice as calm and even as he could.

'But you agree that the source of all magic is Chaos, do you not?' the witch hunter persisted.

'As the mystic winds blow south they separate into their component colours. They in turn are attracted to those parts of the physical environment that share part of their nature,' Gerhart explained, like an impatient temple-school teacher. 'Hence the wind of Aqshy. The source of my wizardry is drawn most readily to the hottest places of the world: fiery, smoke-wreathed mountains, the deserts of Araby or a sun-beaten battlefield in the middle of a drought-laden summer. But a man of your obvious learning and experience concerning the ways of wizards knows this, surely?'

'But do you not agree that all magical power has the capability to corrupt those who wade too deeply in the currents of the sea of dreams?'

Gerhart was quiet for a moment again. 'Yes. I have seen it happen,' he admitted, his shoulders sagging.

'To yourself!'

'No! To others, too many times recently. And one of those was Kozma Himmlisch!'

'You would condemn a dead man? A man you murdered?' Verdammen roared, obviously incensed by Gerhart's words.

'A man I killed in self-defence.'

'So you claim!'

The witch hunter's cold calm had returned and infuriated Gerhart still further.

'It was the astromancer who had been corrupted by the malign influence of Morrslieb. His constant observations of its course through the sky made him mad.'

As he talked, Gerhart continued to worry at the knots behind his back. Contorted muscles, weak from the torture, were now full of the stabbing pains of cramp. He desperately tried to focus and put the pain out of his mind, so he could find a way out of his dire predicament.

He recalled the witch hunter's reaction to his accusation concerning Kozma's state of mind. Perhaps that was something he could use to his advantage? Perhaps he and the witch hunter had something in common. He knew that his own temper was bad but judging by Verdammen's outburst, maybe his anger was also his weakness.

All he had to do was goad the witch hunter into breaking the circle of his wards. Gerhart would be able to do the rest.

He could see the red-orange flickering energies buffeting at the invisible barrier around him.

Then he remembered what else the witch hunter had said.

'I had not realised that you knew Kozma Himmlisch so well... that you had been working alongside him. So you have worked with a practitioner of the very arts you now condemn me for.'

Gerhart glanced from the witch hunter to the crowd and back again to judge the effect of his statement. In the growing gloom of dusk he was just able to make out the disconcerted looks some members of the throng were throwing Verdammen's way.

'Yes, I worked alongside the astromancer,' the witch hunter retaliated, sensing the unease of the crowd, 'as part of an Imperial kommission set up between the colleges of magic in Altdorf and the holy Church of Sigmar, to battle a common enemy. The enemy of all right-minded people – Chaos.'

Gerhart felt the rope loosen.

'But the Kozma I fought was not the same man: he was run mad. What is to say that the corruption he suffered was not shared with those he had been working with?' Gerhart asked innocently.

There was muttering amongst the villagers. These superstitious country folk would believe almost anything, given the right encouragement. They feared witch hunters almost as much as they feared practitioners of the magical arts.

'Watch your tongue, wizard,' Verdammen hissed, taking a step forward, and shaking an accusing finger at Gerhart, 'or I'll have it cut out!'

The wizard glanced down and saw how close the toe of the witch hunter's boot had come to scuffing the edge of the circle of wards. His foot only had to break the circle...

'There is a madness at work here,' Verdammen hissed. 'I have seen signs of it wherever you have been before.'

Gerhart's fingertips tugged at the dangling end of hemp and the knot shifted again.

'I too have seen insanity throughout this province but nothing more insane than this mockery of a trial!'

It was then that Gerhart got the reaction he had been hoping for. But it came much more easily than he had thought, and from a totally unexpected quarter.

The fire mage was suddenly aware of a man running towards him.

'Show some respect!' the henchman bellowed as he rushed over to the bound wizard and struck him across the face with his fist. His stamping feet ploughed through the dirt, scuffing the symbols of warding that had been so carefully inscribed on the ground.

Temper had indeed been the key to free Gerhart.

The wizard found himself at the centre of a vortex of whirling power. The winds of magic rushed into him, just as he pulled a hand free of his bonds.

More than any other, he felt the hot blast of Aqshy
fill him, returning strength to his aching limbs and
abused body. It had found a kindred flame in the
form of Gerhart's boiling anger.

The witch hunter knew he was in trouble. As he
went for the gleaming flintlock pistol at his waist,
he called down all manner of curses on his henchman.

The wizard flung himself onto the ground as the
desperate witch hunter took aim and fired. Gerhart
heard the crack of the pistol, saw the puff of smoke
and felt something whiz past within a hair's breadth
of his scalp. Verdammen's shot had missed.

Crouched on the ground, Gerhart could barely
contain the energy streaming into him. There was
no time to focus and channel the power properly. It
was now or never.

The fires of Aqshy erupted from Gerhart in an
explosion. They were the roiling, hungry flames of a
barely controlled spell.

Possessed of the power of the wizard's temper, the
spell grew into a terrible fireball that blasted out
into the crowd, engulfing everything and everyone
before it.

Standing right in the middle of the spell's path
was the witch hunter. Verdammen didn't even have
time to scream before the fiery conflagration immolated him.

The crowd turned and fled in all directions, running and screaming in panic. The mill caught alight
as the hurtling fireball flew past.

The blazing torch that had only moments before
been Gottfried Verdammen, stumbled away. His
hair and clothes were alight. He emitted a high-

pitched scream from amidst the angry flames, and flailed wildly without sense or reason at any panicked villager who came within reach.

Seeing what had happened to their master, his henchmen turned tail and fled.

Gerhart did not wait to see what happened next. He knew the repercussions that would follow. In the eyes of the people of Hochmoor, everything the witch hunter had told them had just been proved to be true.

Retrieving his sword and staff from the ground outside the magical circle the fire wizard fled into the darkening night. The pyre of the village mill lit up the night behind him with the flickering orange and red light of its destruction.

It was the Great Fire of Wollestadt all over again.

SIX
Council of War

*'With the passing of spring into summer the earth
quickens, the sap flows, blossom gives way to fruit
on the tree, and the Coil of Life surges from the
ground again. Look to the forests and the meadows
and the babbling streams for therein lies our power
and our strength. A man who would forget this and
abandon nature would condemn himself to death.'*

– From Wulfhir's Almanac

BY THE END of spring there was no longer any doubt
that a storm of Chaos was building, the likes of which
no man living had ever witnessed. Word had reached
Wolfenburg of the Chaos hordes cutting a bloody
swathe through Kislev and now the northern borders
were feeling the sting of the enemy's swords. So it was
that as spring gave way to summer, Valmir von Raukov,

Elector Count of Ostland and Prince of Wolfenburg,
called a council of war.

WOLFENBURG.

It sat on a hill, above a bend in the river – a brooding conglomeration of grey towers and walls that
enclosed a myriad of age old buildings. It was a city
that had stood the ravages of time and invading
armies for centuries and had never fallen. Towering
over the ancient city was a castle, an impenetrable
gothic fortress as old, in parts, as the Empire itself.

An air of solemnity hung over the council chamber
of Wolfenburg castle. There was silence as the digni-
taries gathered around the round table, to digest the
news they had just received. The pale-faced messenger,
exhausted from his desperate ride, hovered at the elector count's side on ceremony. He was obviously eager
to be dismissed so that he could retire and get some
much needed rest.

No one spoke for several long, drawn-out seconds. It
was the Lord Chamberlain Baldo Weise who eventually broke the silence.

'Aachden has fallen?' the old man said in astonish-
ment.

'So it would appear,' Valmir von Raukov confirmed,
looking over his shoulder at the messenger who nod-
ded hurriedly in agreement.

'First Zhedevka, now Aachden? Then nothing now
stands between the barbarian horde and our fair city
of Wolfenburg,' Captain Volkgang of the palace guard
opined.

'Quite so.'

The inclement weather that had plagued the people
of Ostland for so many weeks had given way to clearer

skies and brighter, warmer days. With the closing of spring it seemed that summer would open once again like a honeysuckle blossom, golden and sweet.

And yet there had been terrible tales from the north: tales of murder and pillage, of disorder and destruction, of the advance of the servants of evil, of the rise of Chaos.

Valmir von Raukov considered the party seated around the table now. His councillors included men of action but also men of thought. Amongst them were military commanders as well as sagely scholars.

To Valmir's left was Baldo Weise, the elector count's lord chamberlain whose wise counsel had proved invaluable over the years. The grey hair swept back from his balding pate and the severe cut of his beard, combined with the dark look of concern etched on his hawkish features gave the chamberlain an even more stern appearance.

Then there was Siegfried Herrlich, grand master of the knights of the Order of the Silver Mountain, who kept their temple in the city. Siegfried was a soldier of many years experience and an accomplished tactician. In his gleaming armour and mounted on the back of his charger, sword in hand, he made an imposing figure on the battlefield that inspired men fighting alongside him. Out of his armour he was no less imposing: the near white hair at his receding temples and the lines of age that coursed across his drawn and ageing features made him seem distinguished. He was a grandiose figure of authority and nobility, untouched by the negative attributes of old age.

Then there was Captain Franz Fuhrung, commander of the city's garrison. Franz had acquired his position through ability alone, rising through the ranks of

Wolfenburg's army to become captain and be given responsibility for those units of Ostland's standing army that were garrisoned within the city. If Wolfenburg were to come under siege, it would be the soldiers of his garrison that would form the backbone of the ancient city's defence. His uniform was quartered black and white, like the garb his men wore in battle.

Others among the council included the usually taciturn Captain Volkgang of the palace guard, the rough-and-ready Udo Bleischrot, master of the city's guns, and Konrad Kurtz, Wolfenburg's own siege engineer specialist, whose expert knowledge would help the city's defenders, should Wolfenburg be besieged.

At Valmir's right hand sat Wolfenburg's own counsel concerning the matters of magic, the battle wizard Auswald Strauch of the Jade order. The wizard stood out from all the others because of the outlandish garb he wore.

To Valmir he looked like one of the druids that were rumoured to live on the wild island of Albion beyond the dangerous, storm-wracked waters of the Sea of Chaos. His robe was the colour of damp moss and was decorated with a complex pattern of bramble thorns. Leaves were pinned to his cloak and tied with twine to his strong maple staff which rested against the back of his chair, always within reach. The top of the staff bore one of the symbols of the Jade order in beaten copper, the shape of a spiralling coil. Other amulets hung from Auswald's neck on leather cords and gold chains.

The sorcerer had the hood of his robe pulled up, to keep his unruly thick brown hair under control. Like so many who followed the practice of magic Auswald had a thick, bushy beard, nut-coloured and streaked with grey.

From where he was sitting Valmir could see the jade wizard's ceremonial sickle tucked into his belt. Although it was used for certain spells, the sickle doubled as an effective weapon. Valmir knew that Auswald was accustomed to travel about bare-footed, which he claimed helped him to channel the winds of magic.

A notable absentee from the council was Captain Jurgen Enrich, commander of the branch of the knights of the Order of Sigmar's Blood. Captain Enrich had left almost a month ago now. It was hard to predict how long their journey would take, because their progress would be hampered by the horses and oxen that hauled the great gun carriages. Valmir was beginning to wonder if he had been rash in allowing the knights of Sigmar's Blood to ride out with the ancient war banner of the city.

The elector count stroked his long dangling moustaches.

'The time we have been anticipating is almost upon us. I had hoped it would not come, but if Aachden has fallen then Wolfenburg could well be the next target.'

'And there is still no word from Captain Enrich or the cavalcade travelling from Schmiedorf?' Udo Bleischrot asked.

'Sigmar's bones, no!' Valmir growled.

'But they carried the Wolfenburg Standard before them,' Baldo said.

'I know they did,' Valmir said sullenly.

'But legend has it that if the city is attacked without the standard present then it will fall.'

'I know!' Valmir shouted sharply, bringing his clenched fist down hard on the table.

'It's nothing but superstitious nonsense,' Siegfried Herrlich objected.

'Is it?' Valmir snarled, rounding on the grand master. 'The Wolfenburg Standard is one of our city's – and Ostland's – oldest relics. Whatever other powers of protection it may bestow on our bastion's towers and walls, it is a symbol of hope in the face of adversity.'

'Then if it is lost, so shall be the morale of the people. A populace without morale... If that happens then Wolfenburg may as well have already fallen!' Baldo spoke as if thinking aloud.

'Over my dead body!' Valmir bellowed. 'Wolfenburg has stood as a bastion of the Empire's defence for centuries. We have held back the tide of Chaos and repelled those who would ravage the Emperor's realm on more occasions than I care to remember. Why should this be any different? We shall face the enemy and drive them from our lands!'

Valmir was abruptly made aware of a commotion at the door to the council chamber, and a heated, if muffled, exchange of words.

'We shall be ready for whatever the enemy may throw at us, I can assure you of that, my lord,' said Konrad Kurtz.

Valmir could hear the tap of boots on the flagstones of the chamber floor behind him. Doubtless another messenger had been admitted to the chamber.

'We should not worry,' the jade wizard Auswald Strauch said soothingly. 'The standard will protect Captain Enrich and his men. They shall return, and with the cannon train. Then our city will be strengthened, ready to face the enemy and repel them.'

'Is that what you would do? Wait to sit out a siege?' came a gruff voice from behind the elector count.

The council turned as one to see who had invaded their sanctum. Striding towards the table was a lean man, of dishevelled, scruffy appearance, who Valmir judged to be in early middle age. At the stranger's side, and trying to keep up with him, was a man whose livery marked him as a guard captain.

The stranger looked quite similar in overall appearance, and dress, to Auswald Strauch. But where the jade wizard's robes were green the new arrival's were red. Where Auswald's staff was topped with a bronze-beaten badge, the other man's staff was without ornament. In fact it appeared to be burnt at its tip. And where Valmir's sorcerer carried a silver sickle, the newcomer had a scabbarded sword at his side.

The elector count would be having words with this fool of a guard captain who had allowed an armed stranger into his council chamber. But for the time being he would have to let it pass. The arrival of this stranger intrigued him and if the red-robed man tried anything he would soon regret it.

Valmir saw shock, surprise, indignity and suspicion written on the faces of his councillors. He observed their reactions with interest.

'What is the meaning of this interruption?' Siegfried demanded. 'This is a private council of war.'

Others at the table muttered similar responses.

'And a wizard's counsel in war can be as decisive as a soldier's sword,' the stranger said.

'The elector count is already well aware of that,' Auswald piped up. The red-clad wizard turned to face the jade sorcerer, but his expression did not change.

'As you can see,' the elector count said, indicating the jade wizard at his right-hand side.

Valmir saw that Auswald Strauch was scowling daggers at this upstart stranger. He sensed a rivalry between the two already.

'Who are you and how did you get in here?' Valmir asked, his voice as cold as the Kislev steppes in winter, and as sharp as a fractured shard of ice.

'My name is Gerhart Brennend. I am a fire mage of the Bright order, holder of the keys of Azimuth, and I gained entry to this council by telling the guards at the door what I am about to tell you,' the stranger said in a tone of voice that suggested he was used to being listened to.

Valmir stroked his long moustache again and after a moment said, 'Go on then. Tell us what I suspect will be dire news.'

'I have travelled many leagues and braved many perils to warn you of the terrible danger that is facing your city,' said the stranger. 'I believe there is a storm of Chaos brewing to the north, the likes of which has not been seen in the Empire for over three hundred years. It is moving this way and Wolfenburg is directly in its path. The portents tell of impending doom for Wolfenburg, Ostland and even the Empire, unless the tide of Chaos can be stopped in time.

'Many towns and villages have already fallen to the foul machinations of the Dark Powers. A stand must be made here once and for all and I offer you my aid in beating back the enemy hordes.'

'This is ridiculous! I cannot believe what I am hearing!' the jade wizard suddenly blurted out, furiously. 'This vagabond fire wizard is a complete stranger to us – we have no proof of his identity – and he is trying to tell us how to defend our city? He has no business here, no authority. He is intruding on a highly sensitive secret meeting, is he not? By all the gods, he could be anyone. He could even be a servant of the Dark Powers! I demand that he be expelled from this meeting before he does any more to disrupt us!'

'I have defended many settlements from the enemies of mankind and the servants of the dark,' this Gerhart Brennend countered, anger ringing clear in his voice, 'How dare you suggest that I might be one of those black-hearted fiends who follow the fell powers?'

'My lord, please. Throw this man out now!' Auswald persisted.

'Enough!' Valmir bellowed, losing his temper. 'And you would tell your elector count what to do now, would you?' Valmir challenged, raising one eyebrow at his court sorcerer.

Auswald said nothing more – he knew better than to rouse the anger of the champion of Ostland, scourge of the Barbassons and slayer of the Beastmaker. He cast his eyes down. The elector count had made it clear that the matter was in his hands.

'And you,' Valmir said to the fire wizard, 'you march in here, demanding that we listen to you and do as you tell us? You have not told us anything we did not already know. I would advise you that you are only still standing here because I have permitted it. If you have something to share with the council, then tell us. But remember your place, wizard.'

The wizard Gerhart did not looked cowed, and met the elector count's strong gaze with his own. Neither broke eye contact as the fire mage responded to Valmir's chiding.

'I speak not only from my own experiences and discoveries but also from the researches of a noted member of the Celestial order, one Kozma Himmlisch. I speak of plague, mutation, beastmen raids, the malignancy of Morrslieb, and the corruption of good men by the powers of darkness. I speak of a disruption in the winds of magic the like of which I have never known and which chills me to the marrow. Unless we make a stand here against the forces of Chaos, the way will be open for them to march into the middle of the Empire and rip out its heart.'

'You think that we are unaware of this disruption in the flow of the winds of magic, being as close as we are here to the lands of the north?' Auswald blurted out. 'I have already detected this disturbance myself!'

'So what have you done about it?' Gerhart asked, his voice dangerously calm.

It was clear to Valmir that the jade wizard was taken aback by the fire mage's deft riposte. 'What do you mean, what have I done about it? What can anyone do about it?'

'I would have thought someone in your position would have gone on to study what measures could be taken to stop it, or at least to encourage the focus of the winds, or store their energy somehow,' Gerhart explained, his tone still entirely reasonable. 'But I wouldn't want to be telling a court wizard his business.'

'Wolfenburg always stands in a state of readiness,' Franz Fuhrung suddenly spoke up. 'My men are trained and stand ready for anything the enemy might throw at us.'

'We are deeply concerned by the news coming to us daily from the north,' Valmir said, reinstating his authority. 'That is the reason for this meeting and the purpose of this council of war.'

'My lord, I beg your patience,' Gerhart said. Valmir noted that the wizard had remembered to use at least a little etiquette when speaking to an elector count. 'But what counsel has already been given? What, for example, does your court wizard have to say on the matter?'

'The wizard?' Siegfried blurted out, unable to contain himself. 'Why would the prince consult a mage about such matters?'

'I take it he, like myself, is a battle wizard, is he not?' the bright wizard persisted. 'One trained in the ways of war as well as in the ways of sorcery? Is that not so, my lord?'

Valmir turned an enquiring raised eyebrow on the jade wizard once again. 'Well, what would your counsel be Strauch?' he asked.

'I… well…' Auswald stumbled awkwardly.

'Yes?'

'My lord, my counsel would be that we wait for the enemy here. We call the populace from the surrounding environs to join us in the safety of our strong city walls and then we build up Wolfenburg's defences, whilst we wait for the Chaos horde.'

Valmir turned an inquiring look on Gerhart. This fire mage intrigued him. He was obviously in earnest and something about him suggested that the tales he told were more than just words, they were a window on the truth.

'And what would you suggest, wizard? You are eager to hear what others would have your say, what would you advise we do?'

'I would take the fight to the enemy,' the bright wizard said without a moment's hesitation. 'I would rally the forces within your city walls and go out to meet the advancing horde, cutting them off before they have the chance to get dug in.'

'And where did you come by your tactical knowledge?' Valmir asked calmly, yet pointedly.

'I have seen battle in a multitude of arenas, safeguarding our noble Empire from its enemies. I stood

with the host of Eberhardt Eisling at the defence of
Gastmaar Gate. I fought alongside the Averland Harn-
helms at the battle of Morrfenn Field,' the wizard said
proudly, straightening his back and pushing out his
chest. 'I rode with Count Verschalle against the bone-
shard greenskins in the victorious charge of his
Reiksguard Knights. Shall I go on?'

'Yet you would have us act like impatient, impetu-
ous fools and rush headlong to our deaths against the
Chaos horde?' Franz Fuhrung said bluntly.

'Despite your claims it would seem that you are
somewhat deluded concerning matters of war, sir.
Matters which cannot be so easily resolved,' Baldo
said, derision clear in his tone. 'If only they could.'

'What is so difficult about sending trained soldiers
out to fight to save your city?' Gerhart challenged.

'We are down in strength,' Franz said. 'One of our
knightly orders is already on a quest to help bring
reinforcements to our walls. But a reduction in numbers will not matter if we fight from the battlements of
Wolfenburg's mighty walls.'

'Our siege defences will hold the enemy off,' Konrad
Kurtz stated confidently.

'And our own guns will make light work of any siege
engines the enemy might have to threaten us with,'
Udo Bleischrot added gruffly.

'The walls of Wolfenburg will hold.'

'It is as I have already said,' the aging grand master
interposed. 'We should take the fight to the enemy. My
knights are ready to ride at a moment's notice. You
need only give the word, Lord Raukov.'

'This matter is far from resolved,' the elector count
said at last. 'As a soldier, part of me feels that we
should take the fight to the enemy, and yet as lord and

guardian-protector of this ancient city I feel we should stay and face the enemy from a position of strength.'

'My lord–' the bright wizard interjected, but was cut short by gesture from Valmir.

'We have already heard what you have to say, sorcerer. And I must say that your words of warning intrigue me. As a result, you may remain at this council, but there is still much to debate.'

'With respect, my lord,' Auswald Strauch fumed, his face now the same colour as the pyromancer's robes, 'why are we allowing a total stranger a place at this meeting? He should have been expelled as soon as he tricked his way in here!'

'Watch your tongue!' the elector prince snapped with chilling vehemence. 'You would do well to remember your place as well.'

There was a crash and the door to the council chamber burst open. Everyone turned to see who it was that now disturbed them.

'This is preposterous,' Siegfried Herrlich began.

'My lords!' the desperate, sweating messenger gasped as he stumbled to a halt and then remembered to throw the gathered council a bow.

'What in Sigmar's name is it, boy?' Valmir demanded, his chair grating on the flagstones as he pushed it back to stand.

'My lord, one of the knights has returned!' the messenger spluttered.

'One of the knights? The knights of Sigmar's Blood?'

'Yes, my lord. Please come quickly.'

Without further hesitation, Valmir strode from the council chamber.

* * *

THE OBSERVERS STANDING on the battlements of Wolfenburg castle, and on the city's gatehouse, could see the figure galloping towards them in the bright light of the sun. The horse that carried the armoured figure was running hell-for-leather, like a thing possessed. Foamy saliva was flapping from its drawn back lips. It was clear the rider did not have full control of his steed.

That the rider was a knight, that much was clear. He appeared to be riding with his arms outstretched and his head thrown back. As the knight and his terrified steed approached the walls of Wolfenburg along the dusty road the observers could see that the paladin had lost his helmet, and the tabard he wore over his armour was drenched with blood. The stain was so copious that it almost completely obscured the embroidered motif.

It was not until the horse was almost at the gates that the observers saw the crude wooden cross that had been fastened to the horse's saddle, behind the knight. They saw the nails piercing his hands and the blood-soaked ropes around his wrists and neck.

The man had been crucified and was dead.

AND SO IN the days that followed, the ancient city of Wolfenburg prepared for a siege. The people were shaken by the return of the crucified knight. Many on the council of war had felt justified in throwing their support behind the court-appointed sorcerer Auswald Strauch. As, in the end, did the elector count.

Under the direction of Konrad Kurtz, foresters began clearing great tracts of trees that bordered the ancient city, much to the jade wizard's chagrin. But, as it was explained to the incensed sorcerer – who feared such clearing would prevent him from channelling his magic – the trees had to be cut down to remove cover for an attacking force. The cut timber was also needed to fill Wolfenburg's stockpiles of firewood. The boiling of oil, the heating up of the forges, and the like, would also require additional fuel. Nothing would go to waste.

The call also went out to the surrounding towns for reinforcements to aid in the defence of the sentinel city. Messengers were even sent out to the other provinces, as Valmir von Raukov asked his brother elector counts to send troops to bolster the city garrison.

Whilst the council waited for news of help, Udo Bleischrot oversaw the preparation of the city's wall cannons and vase guns. With Konrad Kurtz's support, they prepared other, less technical siege defences such as boiling oil, sling-secured dropping boulders and wall-mounted mangonels.

Meanwhile the forest was being cleared from the front of the city walls.

But despite all the assurances he had been given, the loss of acres of woodland, with its propensity for drawing the wind of Ghyran, filled Auswald with foreboding. Within a week, the jade wizard was sure that he could feel his own power beginning to weaken.

CAPTAIN KARL REIMANN looked up at the imposing walls of the sentinel city through his one remaining good eye. His troop of soldiers crunched to a halt behind him on the stony road. Banners and pennants fluttered from the battlements.

The way to the great gates was choked by masses of peasants who sought shelter. They had abandoned their homes in outlying villages, but whether it was through fear or because they were following the advice of messengers was unclear, but they would be available to fight if need be.

Behind the veteran soldier the road was filling up with more peasant folk and animals. There were also a number of covered wagons, one of which bore the device of the church of Sigmar on its awning. Lone riders gathered amongst the throng.

The Reikland free company, Wallache's Champions, had been among the first to hear of the city's plea for help. Karl's unit had been selected by General Wallache to make its way north, whilst the rest of the company made for Bechafen in the east to fend off attacks by prowling greenskins.

Karl guessed that his soldiers were among the first reinforcements to arrive at Wolfenburg. Certainly their presence in the line had provoked some amount of excitement and discussion amongst the waiting, slow moving throng.

Karl was a figure of imposing Imperial might – his armour was polished until it shone. He had a roaring lion head on his cuirass with the scrolled inscription 'Sigmar' beneath it. His close-cropped white-grey hair, fine moustaches and scarred face lent him a grand air. And the white orb of his blind eye seemed to bore into every man he faced.

If he had not been a humble man, Karl Reimann might have gone as far as to say that the arrival of his unit had filled these desperate, care worn people with hope.

A MERE FIFTY yards further down the road, behind Captain Reimann and his men, a tall figure moved awkwardly among the crowd of jostling peasant folk. He was swathed in a heavy black cloak, despite the warmth of the day. His awkward, shuffling gait suggested that he had been injured in some way. The man travelled alone and made no effort to make himself known.

Instead, as he advanced with the shuffling crowd towards the great gates, and the security they promised, he patted something secured safely beneath his cloak and smiled to himself.

SEVEN
The Siege of Wolfenburg

*'And you shall know the Changer of the Ways by
many names, the Great Schemer, Tchar, the
Master of Fortune, the Great Conspirator, Tzeen,
the Architect of Fate, Chen, Shunch, the Great
Sorcerer, the Great Mutator. For change is all
around us and His schemes and conspiracies are
innumerable but all would bring us to an eternity in damnation.'*

– From the *Liber Maleficium*

THE HIGH ZAR's horde surged over the land in a
ragged tide of death. Scar-marked marauder warriors, wearing trophy arm-rings that attested to
previously won battles, advanced both on foot and
on horseback. Armed with bow, pallasz and spear,
the wild-haired tribesmen made up the bulk of the

army. Leading the marauders were spike armoured giants, the champions of this monstrous force. The great army was comprised of many smaller war-bands, each vying for the favour of the high zar and the Dark Gods themselves. Carynx horns blared amidst the wild, animal shouts of the barbarians and the barking of savage, barely trained warhounds. Their blood was hot and their bloodlust scorched.

Aachden was behind them, gutted like a cadaver on a surgeon's slab, the perimeter to the broken town surrounded by skull stacks and smouldering pyres. The Army of the Reik the high zar's army had faced at Aachden had not merely been beaten – it had been obliterated. A notable victory indeed. Many prisoners had been taken and passed to the slave lord Skarkeetah. All of the zar's warbands had shared in a great, debauched victory feast and the spoils of war divided between them.

But the marauder horde did not luxuriate in the glory of the battle they had won for Lord Tchar. Their blood was up. They felt strong and unstoppable after Aachden, and the ancient city of Wolfenburg was only a few days away. Now that would be an even more worthy conquest for the high zar and the dread lord Archaon! To take the ancient sentinel city would be to take the guts out of the Empire. Their petty rulers and fief-lords would know what true temporal power was when they were begging for their lives on their knees before the Tzeen-blessed form of Surtha Lenk.

'So, THIS IS Wolfenburg,' Surtha Lenk bubbled, gazing out where a forest had once stood to the great grey walls of the closed city.

'It is, lord,' Vendhal Skullwarper confirmed.

'Hmm. I had expected something greater,' the high zar said in his high-pitched voice. 'It is not so different to Aachden.'

'No, lord seh,' the Chaos sorcerer answered, looking out across the cleared slopes. He did so to keep his eyes averted from the high zar.

'It does not look like the men of the Empire want to fight today. No matter, we will take the fight to them, will we not?'

'Of course, lord seh.'

'As we speak my Northmen are preparing the engines that will lay siege to this place. There is still wood enough to do that,' Surtha Lenk said. He was not telling the sorcerer anything he did not already know. He just liked the sound of his own distorted voice. 'We will break this city in a matter of weeks.'

'Perhaps,' Vendhal said cautiously.

At these words, the crimson armoured giant turned to look at the Chaos sorcerer. Vendhal was half aware of the twisted thing squirming in the giant's chest harness.

'Look at me, sorcerer,' Lenk said, all trace of levity gone.

Vendhal turned. Now there was no hiding from the full terror of his lord.

The high zar was a towering giant, a full three spans tall plated in brass and iron with a huge horned, visor-less helm on his head. Strapped across his breastplate was a deformed parody of a human child, all bloated face, warty and blistered, with twitching vestigial limbs.

Even to one as well accustomed to the ways of change as Vendhal Skullwarper, the high zar's appearance was still sickening. It was just such warping mutation that he hoped to avoid through mastery of the warping powers of Chaos.

Surtha Lenk fixed him with a very human brown eye and another bulging, glazed milky-blue orb that spun and twisted in its misplaced watery socket. He was studying the Chaos sorcerer.

Vendhal Skullwarper was clad in his crimson cloak and brass armour, not unlike the high zar's. The hood of the cloak kept the sorcerer's pale face in shadow, so that the tattooed starburst over his right eye could hardly be seen. Gold ornaments glittered in his ears and jewelled amulets hung from his neck.

The sorcerer's upper body was protected by Chaos-forged armour. He wore brass bands emblazoned with the eight points of the rune of Chaos and other blasphemous sigils: all potent devices for drawing the raw power of change to the sorcerer. Spiked iron skull-faces harnessed his cloak to his breastplate and from his belt hung more death-heads and leering daemon mouths fashioned from gold. In one claw-taloned hand Vendhal held his staff of power and in the other an eagled-clawed wand gripped an orb of opaque blue-white crystal.

'What do you mean?' the high zar repeated, his voice dripping with danger.

'The flow of magic is... unpredictable here, lord,' Vendhal replied, choosing his words very carefully.

'But how can we fail? Wolfenburg will be ours. You assured me that your art would make it so.' The horned giant shifted the position of its hands resting on the dreadful blade. 'The touch of Tzeen is upon you, is it not?'

'I have been blessed so,' Vendhal replied, 'but we are far from the Shadow now and the heat of high summer drives its influence back.'

'Our host will drive back the hosts of men and the Shadow will cast its dark magnificence over our endeavours.'

Lenk leaned closer, the shrivelled baby-thing's breath caressing the sorcerer's face. Vendhal gripped his staff more tightly.

'Are not the warping storms of Chaos yours to command?'

'They are.'

'Then the Eye of Tzeen will continue to look upon our enterprise with favour. My battle-shamans will enact the blood-rites that will awaken his power in this place.'

'Of course, lord seh. It will be so.'

'Good, then let us commence. Wolfenburg awaits.'

KONRAD KURTZ WAS standing on the battlements of Wolfenburg's city gates looking out across the cleared expanse of woodland to the distant line of trees on the horizon. There was the enemy.

There were hundreds of them: barbarians, marauders, Northmen, Kurgan and more. These were the foot soldiers of the armies of Chaos, the primitive savages who paid the Dark Gods fealty and who raped, pillaged and murdered in their unspeakable names. They had already put the chill lands of Kislev to the sword and now they were building a road through the northern marches of the Empire cobbled with the skulls of those they had slain.

Konrad could see that the wild-haired, half-naked warriors were gathered together under a multitude of different banners. The brave soldiers preparing to defend the ancient sentinel city stood proud and ready under their own battle standards. Their dazzling coloured cloths became vibrant and alive in the blazing sunlight of high summer. A stiff breeze flapped the flags against their banner poles making the heraldic beasts dance on the fields of cloth, and gold and silver thread-work glitter and sparkle.

Those banners of the barbarians were as barbaric and debased as they were. Their war standards rippled in the wind like ragged shrouds, bloody and corrupted creations of mildewed cloth, flea-ridden animal hides and filth-smeared canvases of human skin.

The sight of them repulsed Konrad. He felt a deep loathing for the Northmen. They wanted to see the ancient guardian city looted and civilisation overturned in favour of their backward culture. Konrad would stand firm against the enemy and play his part in the battle to come, for such a thing must never be allowed to come to pass.

There was unease in Konrad's heart, for there were so many warbands that it appalled the engineer to think that there was one warlord powerful and terrible enough to unite them under a single banner.

It would take a force of terrible strength to conquer this legendary city. Wolfenburg was a fortress town of ancient construction. It occupied a raised hillside above a river bend and it was well fortified. High, solid curtain walls, punctuated at regular intervals by strong towers, were its first line of defence. Beyond these stood further towered walls of great thickness. The city had shut itself up knowing that the Chaos horde was marching this way and it would take the most determined and relentlessly powerful foe to break it open again. This fact alone should have filled the defenders with hope but the memory of Aachden was still fresh in their minds.

A hush had descended over the archers, pikemen and halberdiers lining the walls to Konrad's left and right. Archers and gun crews were at their stations ready to face a siege. Captain Fuhrung's men, clad in their quartered white and black uniforms, were also ready, as he had said they would be. They looked impressive and Konrad knew that the smartness of their uniforms was nothing compared to how they would fight.

Having received word that within two days the Chaos horde would be in sight of the city, the number of men keeping watch from the curtain walls had been doubled. Day or night, the enemy would never be able to take Wolfenburg by surprise. From their vantage point the smoke from the outlying settlements fogged the horizon beyond the trees and served as a warning to them.

Five days earlier, as Konrad and his engineers made their inspection of the battlement defences, the first warbands of the horde had emerged from the distant tree line. And if this was only the vanguard force, as they suspected, the elector count had been right to prepare the ancient city for a protracted siege. No matter how mighty the armies of the Empire might be, the horde that was approaching Wolfenburg was three times the size of the sentinel city's standing force.

'They're planning something,' Udo Bleischrot said gruffly, the stout, soot-stained man approaching the younger, leaner Konrad. The master of the city's guns was wiping his filthy hands on an even filthier piece of grimy oilcloth.

'Surely not another ill-considered assault like last time?' Konrad said, recalling the first attack the Northmen had made against Wolfenburg.

It had been the same day that the wall guards had seen the first flapping banners that had signalled the arrival of the Chaos horde. At dusk the first war-bands, eager to spill blood, launched a hasty assault on the gatehouse, where Konrad and Udo now stood, and the southern wall.

Before the Northmen could even raise ladders to scale the walls they had been repulsed with heavy losses. Udo's vase guns had proved brutally effective whilst hails of arrows fired by the archers on the battlements had rained steel-tipped death on the attackers. Those howling barbarians who made it to the great gates, barred from the inside with a tree trunk, found themselves drenched and scalded by a torrent of oil.

The few survivors of this first assault fled back to the protection of the forest, giving the folk of Wolfenburg time to renew their defences.

Now the Northmen waited, the smoke of their campfires visible during the day, and the flames conspicuous in the darkness at night. But their numbers increased daily as the rest of the horde amassed around them. It was estimated that there were now at least as many as five times the number of barbarians circling the city: bare-chested foot soldiers, horn-helmed horsemen, capering antlered shaman, insane musicians, a cacophony of horn blowers and unrelenting drummers.

That was one of the things that the defenders were finding hard to deal with. The drums beat continually, day and night, and the monotonous pounding was beginning to wear down some of the city's soldiers. The incessant pounding stopped them from sleeping properly. Some of the soldiers watching from the walls now looked just about ready to break and they had barely engaged in any fighting as yet.

It was also uncomfortably hot on the walls of Wolfenburg, but men were reluctant to remove pieces of armour in case of attack. Precious time could be lost if a man was buckling himself back into his cuirass. Instead, grime-faced urchins supplied steady streams of water buckets to the men on watch duty. Every man, woman and child would have their part to play in this siege.

'Yes, they're definitely planning something, the sick daemon-lovers,' Udo said, his eyes half-closed in thought.

'So you think another attack is coming?' Konrad said.

'Something's coming. I can smell it on the wind. They can't sit this one out. It's not their way. If they want Wolfenburg they're going to have to try and take it.'

THE MAIN FORCE of Surtha Lenk's horde set up camp around the city. More wood was cut, but this time by the Kurgan, to feed their cooking fires and construct mobile shields. These same shields were then pushed forward ahead of the horde's archers. This way they were able to get within range of the parapets of the city and repay the blood debt the besieged archers were owed.

The Northmen had gained another addition to their host. They had been building leviathan constructions of wood, iron and tarred hemp. Ranged along the line of trees, the mighty siege weapons looked like monstrous beasts of legend. When they let fly with deadly payloads it was as if dragons and monsters of legend were spewing death down upon Wolfenburg's towering walls.

Sturdy old ballistae, towering trebuchets and taut-roped catapults were aimed at the walls of the city. Sweating teams of Northmen worked tirelessly to ensure that the lethal barrage did not cease.

The ballistae, which were in effect huge siege-proportioned crossbows, hurled heavy bolts of hardwood, two spans long, tipped with cruel iron spearheads at Wolfenburg's solid walls. While the trebuchets and catapults launched boulders, blazing missiles of weighted straw bales, and great flasks of oil boiled on their own fires.

But most horrifying of all to the defenders on the city walls were the rotting human heads. The North-men savages must have collected them after the fall of Aachden and were now using them to demoralise the Empire troops. Nothing put the message across more clearly than having a severed human head thump down on the battlements in the midst of a line of archers. The fleshy skull would roll to a stop at some poor wretch's feet, and its decomposing dead eyes would stare up at him as if to say, 'My fate will be yours.'

Now the siege began in earnest. As the horde's war machines hurled their dread missiles at the walls of Wolfenburg, the city's guns, slings and cannon fired back in retaliation. The resolute defenders even took to launching their attackers' own projectiles back at them. For days the creaking, thumping and squealing of the siege machines could be heard as they launched their deadly cargoes. The thump and crash of the projectiles echoed shortly after.

In reply, the drums of the enemy beat on remorselessly.

The siege ground on day after day, week after week through the sweltering days of the most harrowing summer the people of Wolfenburg had ever suffered.

THE EXPECTED ARTILLERY reinforcements and the Knights of Sigmar's Blood that had ridden out to meet them, had still not arrived.

Some weeks into the siege, Siegfried Herrlich, grand master of the Order of the Silver Mountain, led the full might of his order out of the great gates of Wolfenburg in a sortie against the Chaos warbands. Accompanied by greatswords drawn from Captain Fuhrung's garrison, the two sides clashed on the churned ground beneath the city walls.

The knights and men-at-arms surged out under the banners of the Silver Mountain which depicted a snow-capped peak.

The battle was not without its losses on both sides and as Siegfried Herrlich was heard to declare later that day, when he returned to the sanctuary of the city, 'It felt good to take the fight to the enemy!'

Sorties continued, from time to time, at great cost to both sides. But at least something was being done and it raised the morale of those within the city to see the noble knights-at-arms and the men of the garrison returning to the fold with battle-scars and heroic tales of how they came by them.

* * *

IT WAS NOT only the brave Imperial defenders who became frustrated by the lack of a concise conflict. The Kurgan horde also sought satisfaction in battle, so they too ran out against their enemy.

The warriors of many warbands took part in foot assaults against the solid walls of Wolfenburg, which rose from the bedrock of the hill. They attacked at dusk or dawn, when the treacherous half-light allowed them to get close enough to harry the city walls without being spotted.

When they were within range, the Kurgan archers kept the wall guards busy with sheets of hissing, black-fletched arrows that fell on the battlements in a deadly, stinging hail. As they did so, other marauders charged the walls, protected by the covering fire of the archers' recursive bows. Once at the foot of the battlements, the Northmen hefted their ladders into position, then they would bring up the ram.

The battering ram was a crudely simple yet potentially monstrously powerful weapon. It took teams of straining Northmen to roll it into position, the heavy-wheeled carriage rumbling as it crushed the stones of the road beneath it. Once it was in place, protected by the carriage's portico of stretched animal hide, the Northmen would set the massive timber ram to swing.

These assaults proved costly to the besiegers, however. On several occasions the awning of the ram was set alight by fire arrows or smouldering brands streaking down from the battlements, before it could even reach the gates. Then it had to be withdrawn and the fires doused. To construct another such engine would cost the attackers dear in terms of time, men and resources. If they lost the battering ram their attack would falter and the Northmen would have to withdraw.

When the ram did reach the gates unmolested, it failed to make so much as a dent in the panels of the colossal doors. The rains of arrows, rocks and pitch dropped on them by Wolfenburg's protectors decimated the Northmen scaling the walls. Others died from bone fractures and broken backs, as the ladders they had been climbing were pushed free of the walls.

Such failures did not sit well with the besieging force. They had carved a bloody path across the steppes of Kislev and into the northern reaches of the Empire. Towns and villages had been razed by them, and their march was being halted by this ancient sentinel city. Dissenters began to look for someone to blame. Not enough was being done to end the siege.

There was discord amongst Surtha Lenk's horde.

THE DURATION OF the siege had stretched from weeks into months when Valmir von Raukov, Elector Count of Ostland, called his council of war to meet again. There had been regular meetings between his commanders on a daily basis, of course, but this summons was something special.

Night had fallen and with the watch on the walls and gates doubled once again, they remained undisturbed. A few smouldering torches adorned the walls and candles had been lit in the great cast-iron chandeliers. A waxy smell pervaded the musty air of the council chamber.

There were more men seated at the table than there had been the night Gerhart Brennend's arrival had interrupted proceedings. The fire wizard recognised many of the faces. He was not surprised to find himself excluded from the table; at least he had been admitted to the council meeting.

The fire wizard was not the only observer that evening. Standing around the edge of the hall were men from among the various groups of reinforcements that had heard Wolfenburg's plea and answered it. On this occasion clerics of the religious houses within the city walls had been invited as well: black-robed priests of Morr stood alongside the fur-clad Ulric-worshippers.

Once all were gathered and Elector Count Valmir had addressed the gathering, the current situation threatening Wolfenburg was discussed. Before long a heated debate ensued and the individual frustrations of certain members of the council turned to personal criticisms.

And it was Gerhart Brennend himself who was soon the subject of a number of accusations made by the councillors.

'How goes the defence of the walls?' the elector count asked his captains.

It was Captain Volkgang of the palace guard who answered, and who appeared to have an axe to grind. 'It could have been better. Master Kurtz and Master Bleischrot's siege defences have worked well, but certain people present have been slow to join the battle for our city even though they claim that is why they have come here.'

Gerhart snorted loudly. He had come across Volkgang on several occasions over the last few weeks and already knew what the captain thought of him. He hadn't thought Volkgang would tell tales like a prattling schoolboy with a gripe, however.

'To whom are you referring?' Valmir asked sternly. 'This is a council of war. It cannot operate effectively if we hide behind anonymity and hearsay.'

The blond-haired Volkgang looked across at Gerhart. 'The bright wizard, Gerhart Brennend,' he said. Mutters of agreement rose from various other commanders seated at the table.

'Gerhart Brennend, step forward,' Valmir commanded.

The wizard did so, with a look of reluctance.

'I too was labouring under the misapprehension that you had come to Wolfenburg to help us save our city,' the elector said. 'Is this not the case?'

There were many things the bright wizard wanted to say in response about the city's commanders but instead he said, 'Not at all, my lord. I have taken my place on the battlements during the assaults. But as I have already explained to Captain Volkgang and his fellow commanders,' Gerhart threw his critic a poisonous look, 'the flow of the winds of magic has not been favourable for me.'

'But it is high summer,' Baldo Weise pointed out. 'I would have thought your magic would be at its strongest at this time.'

'And so would I,' Gerhart agreed, 'but the disturbance I spoke of on my arrival, has increased and, if anything, the epicentre of its draining effects have drawn closer to Wolfenburg. It is making the use of magic difficult. There is a danger that any spells cast may be somewhat... erratic, and have an unfortunate effect on our own side.'

'Excuses!' Franz Fuhrung coughed.

'I would not expect a mere soldier to understand the ways of the Artes Magicae,' Gerhart scoffed, his temper rising.

'We have seen little demonstration of this great power you supposedly wield,' Volkgang piped up again, 'and you have had the gall to criticise our choice of tactics, and condemn the course of action decided upon by this council. In fact, you should be battling with us to make it work!'

'Gentlemen, enough!' the elector count said, stepping in before the meeting became a shouting match.

He turned to Baldo Weise, who was seated, as before, at his lord's right hand.

'Lord chamberlain,' Valmir said, his voice having regained its calm tone, 'has there been any more news of the other reinforcements we are expecting?'

'I fear not, my lord,' Baldo said, his countenance as severe as ever. 'It would appear that Baron Gruber's Avengers were the last outsiders to make it through before the enemy cut off any further help from reaching us.'

'There's still no word from Kislev?'

'No, my lord. It appears that they have battles of their own to fight.'

'But what of the cannon train from Schmiedorf?' Valmir persisted. 'I had hoped that some of the Knights of Sigmar's Blood might have survived whatever it was that befell the company. There was a wizard travelling with the cannon-crews, was there not?

'Yes, my lord,' his chamberlain confirmed, consulting a scroll of vellum on the table in front of him, 'of the Golden order: a metallurgist-alchemist by the name of Eisen Zauber.'

'If the Schmiedorf cavalcade could make it as far as the enemy's rear lines, they could break their way through from behind, taking the barbarians by surprise and weakening them at the same time,' Udo Bleischrot suggested, as if thinking aloud. 'Such an action might even lift the siege.'

'Then surely it is imperative that we send a search party to hunt down the awaited reinforcements,' Valmir said, the slightest hint of excitement in his voice. 'A small insertion force, that could evade the enemy outside our gates and travel surreptitiously to its objective.'

'If I might speak freely, my lord?'

'But of course, Captain Fuhrung, go ahead. Speak as freely as you wish.'

'The idea is sound in principle but I cannot spare any of the men from the garrison. Their numbers have been severely depleted by the enemy's attacks and many lie in the infirmary recovering from their injuries and fighting infection.'

'I see,' Valmir said, resting his elbows on the table and steepling his fingers in front of his face. 'Captain Fuhrung, what of the palace guard?'

'It is the same, my lord.'

'My knights are needed here, my lord Valmir' Siegfried Herrlich said, brusquely, before he was even asked.

'Then it would appear that we need to ask our friends, for their help once again,' the elector count said, addressing the men standing at the edges of the room, who listened attentively.

A man who looked every inch the Imperial veteran took a step forward from the throng lining the walls of the council chamber. His hair was grey-white, although to judge by his physique there were still a good few years fighting left in him. The chiselled features of his face bore the scars of battle proudly. The image of a roaring lion head flashed in the light of candles and torches surrounding the walls as he moved out of the shadows where he had stood.

'I volunteer my men for the task,' he said confidently, bowing respectfully to the elector count. Here was a man who was used to the politics of war and court etiquette, as well as its practicalities. 'My men number twenty-two and a more effective regiment of halberdiers you won't find in all the provinces of the Empire, my lord.'

'Thank you... er...'

'Reimann, sir. Captain Karl Reimann of the Reikland free company, Wallache's Champions, sir.'

'Thank you, Captain Reimann, and I gladly accept your noble offer.'

'My men will not fail you, my lord,' the soldier said, saluting.

Another spoke who had remained unnaturally quiet during the proceedings. It was Valmir's court sorcerer, Auswald Strauch.

'My lord Valmir, might I suggest an addition to Captain Reimann's search party?' the jade wizard said.

'Please do,' the elector count replied.

'Considering that Captain Reimann and his men will be running the gauntlet of fell forces who are granted unnatural strength by their unnameable patrons–' At this a number of the priests made the various warding gestures and blessings of their orders. 'It might be wise to send one versed in the magical arts to protect them from the vile warping powers of the daemon lovers.'

Gerhart felt an icy chill crawl down his spine and settle as a knot in his stomach. He knew what was coming before the elector even asked who Auswald Strauch had in mind.

'Why, our honoured guest, Gerhart Brennend who so passionately desires to see our city saved from destruction at the hands of the horde waiting at our gates.'

'An excellent suggestion,' Valmir declared, smacking a hand down on the table. A hint of a smile creased his lips. 'What say you, sorcerer?'

'My lord, my place is in the city,' Gerhart protested. 'This is where I can do most good.'

'But before, you counselled that we should take the fight to the enemy,' Valmir reminded him.

'That was then, my lord. Things have changed since the path of action for this war was decided upon. I really must object!'

'Brennend!' the elector count growled, his tone darkly threatening. 'I would remind you of what I said at our last meeting. You are only here as long as I permit it. You will accompany Captain Reimann and his men on their mission for there are indeed Dark Powers at work and they may well need some form of sorcerous protection on their journey. Do you accept, or shall I have you accused of treason and deal with you accordingly?'

Gerhart knew when he'd been beaten. Anger with the jade wizard seethed beneath his calm exterior. What was Strauch doing? Men of their measure should work together to support one another. Did he not appreciate this? Valmir's court sorcerer had obviously never met a man like Gottfried Verdammen.

'I accept, my lord.'

'Good. Then I see no reason for any further delay. Captain Reimann, you will prepare to leave at once.'

'Just one question, my lord,' Gerhart said, speaking up again.

'What is it?'

'How will we get out of the city without being seen by the enemy?'

'Don't worry,' said Konrad Kurtz, Wolfenburg's own siege specialist. 'Leave that up to me.'

'HERE IT IS,' Konrad said, pointing at the culvert and the dressed stone arch, no more than a span high, in the wall of the dungeon chamber.

The thin, low tunnel looked just like a drain. The tiles lining it were wet with algae and there was a steady trickle of water inside it. In the flickering torchlight Gerhart could see nothing but blackness.

'This is it?' the wizard said, aghast.

'This is it,' Konrad confirmed. 'Don't worry. As the tunnel starts to descend, so the roof rises. You'll be able to make most of your way walking upright.'

'And this will lead us right out of the city?' Karl Reimann asked. His men were ready, waiting behind him in a huddled line.

'The tunnel runs for almost two miles. It emerges through a natural cave at the base of a wooded hill to the south. Our observers on the walls say that the trees there have been left untouched. The nearest Northmen camp appears to be a good half-mile away, between Wolfenburg and the tunnel's exit. You should be able to evade the Chaos forces without great difficulty.'

'Thank you, my friend,' Karl said, shaking hands firmly with the siege engineer.

'Here, you'll need this,' Konrad said, handing the soldier a shuttered lantern.

Karl climbed down into the culvert.

'Good luck.'

'By Thyrus Gormann's beard, something tells me we're going to need it,' Gerhart said, as he stepped down into the drain and disappeared into the dark.

EIGHT
Shadows of the Forest

*'Out in the shaden wodespan, dwelt the
murdrus beaste,
Vittalling on the sack-for-homes, gorge-laden
with his feaste…
And noth there was that brave the woode,
Noth amidste the sword-handy and the goode.'*

– From the nursery tale of the Empire,
'Tomas Wanderer'

AT FIRST IT appeared as if the village of Walderand was
just like all the others Wilhelm Faustus and his followers had come upon since reaching the lands
surrounding Wolfenburg. A settlement such as this
one, lying as it did on the edge of the forest, should be
alive with the sounds of bustling villagers, the lowing
of cattle, the bleating of sheep and goats, the chop of

the axe on wood, the sluicing of water drawn from the stream, the rumble of grinding millstones and the ringing of the blacksmith's hammer on the anvil at the village forge. But there wasn't a single sound of civilisation.

All that could be heard was the mournful croaking of black-winged carrion birds roosting in the treetops of the encroaching woodland and the babbling of the village brook, which to Wilhelm sounded more like a sinister whispering. It was as if unseen spirits were watching his warband's progress and relaying what they saw to whatever was lurking in the depths of the forest.

It was high summer. No breeze blew, the air was still. But still the musky scent of the beast was carried to the warrior priest's senses. The village nestled amongst low wooded hills within a shallow valley. The straggly edge of the Forest of Shadows stood on the far side of the incline to the east of Walderand, beyond the boundary of outward-pointing sharpened stakes.

Lector Wilhelm Faustus and his growing entourage had reached Wolfenburg, but they were already too late, and soon realised the futility of their enterprise. The awaited fearsome enemy, the hosts of the Northland tribes, had descended on the city and laid siege to it. The numbers of the enemy forces were terrible to behold: bow-trained horsemen, marauding foot soldiers, siege weapons of ancient magnitude, gigantic champions clad in cruelly-barbed plate mail, smoky-breathed warhorses and worse things too.

They had looked down on the grey sprawl of the city, held in check within its ancient solid curtain wall, and seen the Northern tribesmen disfiguring the landscape with their mere presence. Where the barbarians had made camp, the lush green meadows had become marred, black, brown and grey by the corrupting influence that followed in their wake.

Although his entourage had been growing steadily ever since he left Steinbrucke until it numbered somewhere in the region of fifty good souls, Wilhelm did not consider them ready to face the savage, blood-crazed warriors of the North. Wilhelm's followers were not trained fighters and many were no longer in the prime of life, either due to ill health or old age, and there were only so many visions of hell that the common man could endure before his mind fractured under the sheer horror of it all.

With every village, country estate or hamlet they visited, with every victory Wilhelm claimed in Sigmar's name, the numbers of his followers grew. The desperate, the distressed, the dispossessed, the penitent and the pious; they were all drawn to his cause, until the wandering band of holy servants of Sigmar had become comparable in size to that of a free company. It was a small army of flagellants, zealots and fanatics.

Wilhelm caught another whiff of the musky animal scent. He thought it likely that the population of Walderand had either fled or been massacred in their homes, just as they had in a dozen or so other places he had encountered already. Clicking his tongue, the warrior priest resumed his ride towards the heart of the village.

It was then that he heard the pitiful, plaintive cries. He only had to ride a little further to discover what had befallen the people of Walderand.

The villagers had been penned inside a stockade corral of sharpened tree-posts four spans high as if they were cattle. The people looked haggard and dishevelled, as if the fight had been beaten out of them. None of them seemed in any fit state to attempt a breakout either – how long had they been kept penned up like this?

There was indeed a very good reason why none of them had attempted to break out.

Standing outside the corral were two ugly, inhuman brutes. Each was at least a head taller than the warrior priest who was considered tall amongst other men. Their bodies were covered with matted fur, and caked in mud and dung. They had broad barrel chests and their strong arms were corded with muscle. They stood on backward-jointed legs that looked like the hindquarters of stags, and their feet were cloven hooves. Their loins were covered by scraps of cloth and torn chainmail and around their necks clattered necklaces of human bones. Each creature held a brutal-looking weapon: one a broad-bladed axe and the other a great gutting pallasz. Rising from their thick bull necks were blunt-snouted goat-like heads, with curling horns above their caprine skulls.

Wilhelm Faustus knew these children of Chaos for what they were. He had dealt with their kind many times in the past. These were beastmen, and he knew how to deal with them.

On seeing the ugly, malformed brutes parading before him in bestial arrogance, reason left the lector priest for a moment.

He gave a shout of, 'In Sigmar's name!' and kicked Kreuz into a gallop, charging straight towards the foe. He held his steed's reins tightly in his right hand, along with his battered shield and swung his warhammer into a more comfortable position in his left. The muscles of his arm bulged, but the priest wasn't aware of the strain. He kept his body in the peak of fitness in order to serve the Heldenhammer.

Hearing Wilhelm's shout the two beastmen immediately turned their beady, animal eyes on him. They grunted and huffed at one another, the noises like those of swine or cattle. Hefting their own weapons they stepped forward to face his charge. These were not creatures to shy away from a challenge.

As he drew closer to the beasts, Wilhelm picked out distinctive differences between the two. The one to his left had an eight-pointed star rune described by scars cut into the flesh of his torso. It stood out now, knotted and black. The second, to his right, had four rams' horns curling from its brutish head rather than two, like its fellow.

The Chaos-rune marked beast ran forward, raising its axe as if to take Wilhelm's warhorse down with a slashing cut from the knock-edged weapon. Kreuz whinnied wildly and reared up on his hind legs. The priest held on with his hand tight on the reins, gripping his steed's sides tightly between his thighs. At the same time he brought his hammer round in a circle and smashed the beastman's axe away.

The animal snarled and stumbled sideways, unbalanced by the priest's resounding blow. It howled as Kreuz's sharp-edged, iron-shod hooves came down on its back as it turned, trying to regain its balance. Chaos-scar stumbled further away.

Wilhelm could hear the eager shouts of his entourage as they too charged into the village, following his lead. Leaving the bolder of the beast guards to the zealots, Wilhelm charged his steed towards the second brutish savage.

Four-horns might not have been so bold as Chaos-scar but neither was it so brash. As the priest galloped towards it, the beastman deftly sidestepped, delaying its two-handed thrust with its pallasz until Wilhelm was already half past the creature's position. Wilhelm had to suddenly defend himself with his shield, bracing himself against the blow. The heavy pallasz rang on the battered metal of the shield but Wilhelm kept his seat in the saddle.

Before four-horns could raise its weapon fully again, Wilhelm swung Kreuz round so that the beastman was now on his left-hand side. He brought the warhammer down with a mighty swing and caught the beast a glancing blow with the edge of the hammer's head, tearing open the muscle of its calf. Four-horns gave a guttural bark and lurched sideways.

The beastman rammed into the priest's horse with its shoulder causing Kreuz to take several faltering steps to his right. But the warhorse was strong too. Kreuz retaliated by swinging his chainmail barded head at four-horns. It was obvious that the beastman had not been expecting such a reprisal. It reeled away, bringing it within open range of Wilhelm's hammer again.

The priest and his warhorse made a formidable team, as many a foe had found out to their cost, just before they died.

The lector struck again. He heard the crack of bones breaking as his hammer struck the beastman's shoulder. Blood spurted and the beastman howled.

Wilhelm struck again.

This time the brute went down on one knee. The warrior priest's blow had shattered the bones of its elongated ankle. White splinters could be seen through the ragged red of its ruptured flesh as the broken bone burst through the skin.

The avenging Sigmarite struck once more. The flat head of his warhammer slammed into the upturned snout of the creature, smashing the shattered bones of its skull back into its brain. The beastman collapsed to the ground and lay motionless, face down in an expanding pool of its own dark blood.

Certain that the beast was dead, Wilhelm looked back to where a group of his followers had fallen on Chaos-scar and were hacking the dying creature apart with spear and sword.

Pride swelled in the warrior priest at the sight. Sigmar's work had certainly been done here today.

In the few minutes that Wilhelm fought the beast guards, the broken villagers had remained silent, too shocked and stunned to do anything else. Now that the battle was over, however, and they saw the small army following in the warrior priest's wake, the imprisoned villagers broke out into an excited chattering, many offering up prayers of thanks to Sigmar and his wrathful prophet.

Amongst all the clamour Wilhelm caught snatches of other phrases being called out by the villagers: words that sounded suspiciously like 'trap' and 'ambush'.

'Release them,' Wilhelm instructed, indicating the penned people. 'Find them something to eat and drink and have those skilled at healing tend any who are injured.'

With the help of Walderand's villagers, the priest's entourage began to dismantle the stockade. Wilhelm dismounted as the first of the prisoners was released.

The stick-limbed man stumbled over to him in a state of anxiety.

'Thank Sigmar, you found us in time!' he said, grabbing the warrior priest's gauntleted hand and shaking it vigorously in a double-handed grip.

'I thank Sigmar for that too,' the priest boomed.

Wilhelm looked over the man's shoulder to see how the others were faring after their ordeal. Then he sharply turned back to the man still shaking his hand.

'You must get out of here!'

'What do you mean? And what did you mean by "in time"?'

'Before the others return. You have walked right into their trap!'

'Sigmar's bones!' the priest cursed, leaping back into the saddle. How could he have been so foolish? 'Arm yourselves!' he bellowed both to his entourage and to the villagers. 'This isn't over yet!'

And then he heard it: a clattering of metal, accompanied by a braying cry and the crash of splintering wood.

The beastman herd emerged from the straggly edge of the forest banging their weapons against crude, skin-drawn shields. Wilhelm and his entourage, hurriedly forming up into ranks, could see the beasts quite clearly, as they pawed the ground at the top of the slope.

Wilhelm reckoned there were almost as many beastmen among the tribe as there were men in his party. Every one of them, even the more human-seeming creatures with only small stumps of horns protruding from their thick, overhanging brows, would be more than a match for one of the Emperor's trained soldiers. Many of Wilhelm's holy entourage were not trained soldiers. He would simply have to pray that their holy zeal would take them to victory, for how could the warped and twisted parodies born of Chaos conquer an army of the warrior god Sigmar?

'Prepare for battle!' Wilhelm shouted to the army amassed behind him. 'Look to the Heldenhammer for your strength and courage and we cannot fail!'

Wilhelm saw a goat-headed creature in the front line of the enemy horde put a long, curling horn to its malformed lips. The vibrating, mournful note it produced resounded across the field of battle now formed between the two sides. A roar went up from the herd and the beastmen advanced en masse.

Now Wilhelm understood why the villagers had been corralled within Walderand, and the reason for the two lone guards. His progress had been watched. The villagers had been bait, their guards a mere distraction. And Wilhelm had been duped. Animal cunning had won out over human intelligence.

The beastmen surged towards Walderand like a crimson tide; the creatures' hides a ruddy-brown colour, their horns daubed with blood and red ochre. The one creature that stood apart was a colossal, dark-skinned monstrosity. It was fully three spans tall and its dye-stained horns rose to another span above that. This creature was obviously a champion among its kind, a wargor, marked out for greatness by the Dark Gods in whose unspeakable names it slaughtered and maimed. In its hands it held what looked like the broken axle of a chariot, with a long curving blade attached to the hub of the now broken wheel.

The champion gave a guttural bellow which could be felt as much as heard over the whooping and braying of the herd. It vibrated in Wilhelm's belly. The beastmen broke into a canter. The herd's vanguard reached the staked defences as Wilhelm's own force moved forwards. Several of the more human-looking creatures hurdled the village's defences, landing amidst the holy entourage. The battle had begun.

Wilhelm swung his hammer and broke the neck of an ape-snouted creature that lunged at him. As he continued the swing, ready for his next strike, he lashed out at another of the mutants with the edge of his shield. The creature fell back, a deep red gash opened across its ribs. The crude spear it had thrust at the priest fell to the ground, and the ungor fell beneath the trampling hooves of a larger, longer horned gor.

The beastmen fell on the weaker humans in a frenzy of savage bloodlust.

The men of the lector's troop and some of the villagers too, fought back admirably, but it was clear who had the advantage. The beastmen had been raised to fight from birth. It was central to their existence. If they weren't fighting the people of the Empire, or raiding from their forest lairs, they were battling other tribes for the best hunting grounds, or even fighting amongst themselves to maintain the hierarchical structure of the tribe. And whilst the humans' weapons were, on the whole more refined and better engineered than those of the herd, the beasts didn't need to rely on weapons alone. They used their horns, their claws, their hooves or their teeth.

A wargor sank its filthy fangs into a flail-wielding zealot's arm. The man screamed and dropped his weapon, only seconds before the monster tore the man's arm out of its socket in a great gout of blood, and a sharp jerk of its head.

Another beast put its head down and charged a greatsword who had joined Wilhelm's wandering crusade outside Haargen. The soldier hacked at the gor with his blade but it simply scraped off the hard prongs of the creature's horns. These same horns then impaled his stomach. The beast shook its strong neck and the greatsword's midriff was torn open, the purple cords of his entrails spilling free in a torrent of blood.

Cries of anger and dismay suddenly went up from a group of flagellants as a crude rattling chariot charged across the battlefield at breakneck speed. Resembling nothing more than several large pieces of lumber nailed and strapped together, it was drawn by two hulking creatures that looked like wild boars mutated into huge horned and tusked monsters.

The tuskgors – for that was the name these warped animals were known by – ploughed through the ranks of the Sigmarite army, dragging the shaking chariot behind them. They crushed any who got in the way of their heavy hooves or the iron-banded wheels of the wheeled platform they hauled.

One man was impaled on the horns of one of the tuskgors and then tossed high into the air as it threw its head back. The unfortunate wretch landed amidst a pack of ravening, battle-frenzied ungors that proceeded to tear him limb from limb.

Smashing another beast-creature to the ground with his now flame-wreathed warhammer, Wilhelm took stock of the battle. What his men lacked in formal weapon training they made up for in sheer zealous aggression and determination.

Close by a man was whimpering, half his face was hanging off as he had been dealt a vicious blow by a cleaver-weapon. The human fighters were being cut down by axes and huge gutting knives. Arterial blood was fountaining into the air from stumps of limbs and half-severed necks. Something that might once have been either a wolf or a wild dog took down a half-armoured flagellant and tore off his head with distended, crushing jaws.

The priest knew that he had to do something or the battle would be lost. He kicked out, and planted his foot in the pug-face of one of the lesser beastmen, booting it aside. He turned Kreuz towards the beast-man champion that was cutting a bloody swathe through the ranks of his army.

The shaggy-haired, goat-headed abomination wore the curve-horned skull of another of its kind on the belt about its waist. No doubt the skull had belonged to a rival this monster had bested in combat to become the wargor champion. However, the goat skull was not only a sign of the beastman's status, it could also be used as a weapon.

As Wilhelm bore down on the beast the creature thrust itself towards an unfortunate halberdier, taking the man's eye out and ripping off half of his face. At the same time he beheaded the man behind with the blade of his chariot axle.

'Against the children of Chaos we trust in the light of Lord Sigmar!' the warrior priest exclaimed and, with the holy power of the Heldenhammer surging through his every fibre, he struck the champion's weapon a ringing blow. What was left of the axle shaft splintered in two and was knocked from the monster's grip.

The wargor grunted but before it could react Wilhelm had struck again. A flash of light burst from the head of his hammer as he did so and the beast howled in pain as the searing golden glare blinded it. As the creature flailed with its filthy talons in front of its face, Wilhelm struck again and again.

Neighing wildly, Kreuz reared up on his hind legs and crashed his hooves down upon the great barrel chest of the beast. The wargor stumbled backwards and toppled over completely. There was a sickening crunch, like a pumpkin being pronged by a pitchfork, and the tips of sharpened stakes burst through the creature's face and torso.

Wilhelm had not realised how close to the outskirts of the village his charge had taken him. The blinded beastman had been driven back onto the staked defences erected on Walderand's outskirts.

A howl went up from the nearest beastmen that was soon taken up by the rest of the herd. Their champion was down, slaughtered like a beast in an abattoir. It was just the breakthrough Wilhelm's entourage needed.

The herd broke apart in panic, turning from the battle and bounding back to the cover of the darkly brooding woodland. At first only the ungors fled from the battle. Then their larger cousins, seeing their numbers dwindling against the increasingly incensed attacks of the humans, also turned tail and ran. Within moments the beastmen were gone, their hoots and brays echoing back through the trees to the ears of the victorious Sigmarites.

Lector Wilhelm Faustus's victorious rabble were not prepared to leave it there.

'The enemy are in rout,' someone yelled.

'This is not over until we have run to ground every last one of the foul beasts,' a flagellant shouted.

'Not one of the twisted spawn must be left alive!' echoed another.

Paying little heed to the dead and dying who lay on the blood-soaked meadow, those still in a condition to fight followed the dwindling cries of the beastmen into the encroaching forest, straight into the beasts' own territory.

'Sigmar's teeth!' Wilhelm cursed, his breath coming in great heaving gasps after his exertions.

If he was to save what remained of his zealot army, the warrior priest knew what he had to do, even though the thought of such an action went against his better judgement. Pushing Kreuz to gallop once more, Wilhelm drove his steed up the slope and into the green gloom of the forest, the domain of the beastmen.

BENEATH THE TREES it was as dark as dusk. Wilhelm left Walderand behind as he penetrated the twisted depths of the primeval forest in pursuit of his over-zealous entourage and the beastmen. He could hear the shouts of the men who had sworn to follow him into battle against the hordes of evil receding into the distance.

Just for a moment Wilhelm Faustus wondered if he had been a little too hasty to pursue his men and the routed herd. Perhaps he had allowed his religious fervour to drive him to recklessness in his determination to purge the land of the children of Chaos. He had rushed headlong into the woods on the heels of his entourage just as they had raced after the fleeing beastmen. This was the beasts' territory after all.

This was the Forest of Shadows, a vast expanse of ancient, untamed woodland. Legends and rumours abounded about the place, about what was supposed to lie within its haunted depths. There were tales of greenskins and mythical Chaos-warped leviathans of another age, along with stories of beastmen encampments and long-forgotten barrow mounds.

It seemed that the beasts had vanished after entering the twisted tangle of trees and dense undergrowth. The lector could no longer hear the sounds of the fleeing herd that had crashed through the undergrowth, hollering and braying.

Wilhelm abruptly reined Kreuz to a halt. He heard a rustling from somewhere in the darkened canopy above him and looked up.

A beastman came crashing down on him from the branches of the tree. The full weight of the feral creature collided with the priest, knocking him out of the saddle and onto the root-knotted ground. Panicked by the sudden attack, Kreuz bolted off into the trees.

Wilhelm tried to pick himself up as the beastman rolled aside, only to find himself surrounded by more of the degenerate creatures, ungors and their larger goat-headed cousins. The warrior priest reached for his holy weapon.

'Sigmar's hammer!' he cursed, his voice booming between the twisted trees over the jeering snarls and whoops of the beasts.

Once again it seemed that brute cunning had won out over human courage and intelligence. He was surrounded and horribly outnumbered, in the territory of the herd, cut off from all other help.

Wilhelm began to form a prayer to Sigmar to call down his patron's divine wrath upon the foe. He raised his consecrated weapon to smite the nearest of the animals.

He heard the crack of the spear-shaft striking the back of his head before he blacked out and then he was aware of nothing more.

NINE
Chaos Ex Machina

'When asked, What is the name of the noblest
of metals?
Thou shalt respond: "Gold".'

– From *The Training of the Alchemist*
by Balthasar Gelt

THE PARTY HAD been travelling for several days and had
cleared the enemy cordon surrounding Wolfenburg.
Just as Konrad Kurtz had promised, the secret tunnel
leading from the dungeon in the castle had brought
them out south of the city, at the foot of a wooded hill.
The nearest Northmen camp was roughly half a mile
away.

As the soldiers emerged from the narrow cave-mouth
into the twilit summer night they saw the flickering
glow of camp-fires and heard the bestial carousing of

the Chaos forces as they readied their weapons for war, or paid homage to their foul pantheon of Dark Gods. As far as the wizard and the Imperial soldiers could tell, none of the enemy host had seen them.

They had moved as quickly and as quietly as they could, keeping to the cover of grassy hummocks and straggly trees growing from the uneven ground. After a couple of miles of cross-country travel, Captain Reimann had led the party onto the road and the speed of their progress improved. Just before dawn they had rested within the depths of a dense coppice, with at least two men keeping watch at all times.

If at all possible they wanted to try to avoid any encounters with the enemy at such an early stage. They were one regiment supported by one wizard after all, and they had no idea how far they might have to travel before they found the missing cannon train. And even then they had no idea what they would have to deal with when they did find it – if they did.

They were travelling steadily south-west, towards Schmiedorf a distance of seven leagues from Wolfenburg all told. They had two scouts ahead to warn of anything approaching on the road. They had seen neither hide nor hair of any forces, Imperial or heathen, in all that time. However, neither had they seen any sign of the cannon train or the Templar knights that had been sent to escort the guns to Wolfenburg. Too much time had passed for there to be any tracks left to read on the road.

The journey had been a quiet one. Karl Reimann's men engaged in occasional muttered conversation but they never included the wizard. He knew they were wary of him, and uneasy about having him in their party. The only time their captain spoke to him was when he wanted Gerhart's opinion on a suggested course of action, or if he wanted the wizard to read the flow of the winds of magic and warn them of approaching danger, which wasn't often.

As they trudged on Gerhart found himself considering what would happen on their return to Wolfenburg. If they were able to complete their mission and make it back to the beleaguered city he doubted very much that the tunnel would still be open to them. In all likelihood it would have been blocked, in case their exit had in fact been observed by any of the Chaos troops.

Besides, Gerhart thought, with a glimmer of untypical optimism, if they completed their mission they would not need to use the tunnel to make it back into the city. They could simply blast their way through the enemy lines with the recovered cannons.

'Captain, look at this,' one of the halberdiers said.

The soldier's commanding officer moved to where the man stood. They were currently following the road to Schmiedorf through a rocky defile. Grass-tufted cliffs of limestone rose up thirty feet on either side of them. There was no mistaking the signs of what had happened here. The black soil of the road at the bottom of the gorge was churned with hoof-prints and parallel gouges, which looked like wheel marks. Although it had probably rained since the marks were made, they were still very deep.

'Well at least we know what happened to the cannon train,' Gerhart said gruffly from the back of the huddle of men.

'You think this was them?' Reimann asked as he poked and prodded at the churned ground.

'I think it very likely.'

'It was an ambush then?'

'I would say so. There were no such marks further back up the road. I expect whoever attacked them launched their attack from the top of this gorge, blocking their way forward and then following through with an assault from behind,' Gerhart said, scanning the sides of the gorge around them. 'There would have been no way the guns could have been brought to bear and obviously their escort, knights or no, were overwhelmed.'

'You said "whoever" attacked the cannon train,' Karl pointed out, picking up on the precise words the wizard had used. 'It was the enemy, surely.'

'It may well be but we can't be sure yet,' Gerhart replied.

'If you are sure it was the cannon train how can you not be sure it was ambushed by the enemy?' the veteran infantryman persisted.

'I said I thought it was likely that it was the cannon train that had been attacked here.' The fire mage fixed the captain with a beetling black stare. 'You would do well to remember that there are other things that prey on travellers in these parts.'

'Very well,' Karl conceded. 'But where are the Schmiedorf cannons now?'

'That is what we need to find out,' Gerhart replied.

'And where are the bodies?' Karl added, as if the thought had only just dawned on him. 'Why would the ambushers have taken them?'

'Now that, captain, is a good question,' the wizard said thoughtfully.

How could he have not realised earlier? There had been so little traffic on this road that it seemed unlikely that anyone else would have moved the corpses, had they found any. It certainly wouldn't have been the work of scavengers: animals would have gnawed upon the bodies where they found them. There would have been body parts and clothing, weapons or armour left behind. Even if they had been looted, there would have been still evidence that someone had died here. And if there had been any survivors surely their own party would have encountered them by now.

For all the cannon train's entourage to have been taken, the dead as well as the living, and their horses, suggested to Gerhart that this could indeed have been the work of a Chaos warband. Possibly greenskins, but it all seemed too well organised.

'The cannon train was attacked, its defenders overcome, and then everyone and everything was hauled away,' he said.

'So what do we do now?' one of the halberdiers asked.

'The guns may well still be intact, in which case they can be recovered,' Reimann said with confidence. 'Von Raukov himself laid the responsibility of this mission upon us. He commanded us to hunt down the missing reinforcements. We might have found signs of them, but so far we have not found the cannon train itself. Our mission is not over until we have determined its fate and done what we can to rectify the matter. So, we follow these tracks back and see where they lead us.'

KARL'S HALBERDIERS CONTINUED as they had before, with the bright wizard in tow, following the trail left by the captured cannon train as it wound its way up into the surrounding hills. They kept low as they moved over the ground, always looking out for the enemy. These hills were only the foothills of the Middle Mountains, whose imposing peaks were still snow-capped even in the middle of summer.

It was the wizard who first noticed the distant smoke. In fact, he seemed to be aware of it before the rest of them. Karl guessed his enhanced senses were linked to the eldritch powers at the wizard's command.

At first the rising smoke was a barely visible charcoal line against the cerulean blue of the cloudless summer sky. After half a day's travel Karl's troop of soldiers could all see it clearly: a column of grey dissipating into the atmosphere, unruffled in the still air.

The following morning, as they crested a chalky peak among the craggy hills, it became quite clear that the clouds of thickening smoke were rising from a point not far away. Their quarry was within reach at last, Karl was sure of it.

Yet still they had seen no sign of anyone, friend or foe. This state of affairs would change very soon, the old veteran was certain.

'THERE IT IS,' the halberdier captain said in a harsh whisper as the party peered over the lip of the precipice.

Gerhart Brennend, lying on his front next to the veteran peered over the edge of the cliff into the quarry. Karl Reimann had been correct in his initial assumption as to who had attacked the cannon train. The Chaos encampment appeared to have been set up within the open, chalky scar of an abandoned stone quarry at the heart of the hills. Of course, whether it had been abandoned when the

warband and its prisoners had arrived Gerhart had
no way of knowing.

This camp was very different from those of the Kurgan host outside Wolfenburg. For one thing Gerhart
didn't believe that these followers of the Dark Gods
were Northmen marauders. This warband was quite
different to the tribal gatherings of the barbarians.
Gerhart knew there were wandering warrior bands that
had dedicated themselves to the service of those
malign entities that would see creation unravel under
their influence, and they had never travelled beyond
the realm of the Empire. He had fought such warbands in his days as a battle-wizard.

Figures in spiked armour moved amongst the flickering fires that cast an orangey glow on the quarry
walls. The Chaos warriors were clad in black armour
embellished with brass and gleaming iron. The plate
mail was ornamented with sharp arrow points, leering, fang-mawed iron skulls, spikes and dagger-blades.
Their narrow-slitted visors were adorned with curving
horns much like those favoured by the Northmen
marauders. The Chaos warriors' weapons were of
superior quality, huge, and heavy and deadly sharp
blades. Many possessed long shields again adorned
with the symbols of their blasphemous gods.

Some of the Chaos warriors were putting their huge
curve-bladed axes to work chopping up wood of other
gun carriages and wagons to fuel the fires built around
the encampment.

The wizard's party had come upon the Chaos camp
as night was falling and suddenly all their questions
were answered. The remnants of the cannon train lay
at the centre of the ruined quarry workings. Gerhart
was appalled to see that a number of the great guns

had been destroyed, either dismantled or blown apart, probably with the barrels of gunpowder that had been carried with the cannon train. Several large pieces of blackened, twisted and melted lumps of iron lay around the quarry camp. A makeshift forge had also been erected, possibly utilising equipment that the Schmiedorf cavalcade had brought with it.

Had the great cannon made it to Wolfenburg, the wizard was sure they would have broken the Northmen's siege of the city.

The insane daemon-worshippers had not destroyed all of the ancient weapons. One monstrous cannon stood on its wooden wheeled frame at the centre of the quarry. It was at least five spans in length and as tall as a man. It must have been the greatest of the Schmiedorf guns, but now it looked little like the mighty Imperial weapon it had once been. Huge metal spikes had been driven into the belly and barrel of the cannon. It had been banded with belts of ruddy brass, and strange shapes, possibly letterforms, had been engraved into the metal.

Gerhart looked away, his eyes stinging and gorge rising in his throat.

Chaos runes, he thought. Their blasphemous form twisted the very fabric of reality around them and made them unbearable to look at.

Not too far from where he was lying Gerhart heard one of the soldiers lose the contents of his stomach. He too must have looked too long upon the hellish graffiti etched into the great gun.

This wasn't all the Chaos warband had done to transform the cannon. The last remaining survivors of the party that had set out from Schmiedorf had been bound with chains to the body of the foul construction. The men were bloodied and beaten, but they were not dead. The bright wizard had a horrible suspicion that the warband was intending to use the men as sacrifices.

Amongst those strapped to the massive cannon was one man who stood out thanks to his attire. Gerhart could see the tendrils of power writhing around him. The man had luxuriant blond hair and a beard of yellow-gold curls. His tattered yellow robes were made of a material that sparkled and shimmered as it reflected the incandescent glow of the fires. The sigils and runes embroidered on the cloth reflected back to Gerhart.

This poor wretch could only be one man: the metallurgist-sorcerer of the Golden order who was supposed to have been travelling with the cannon train: Eisen Zauber.

Surveying this work was the overseer of this particular warband. The creature stood on an outcrop of rock, looking down on the mutilated form of the great cannon. He was tall and lean, easily as tall as the armour-clad warriors. His entire body was covered in a robe of strange, shifting-hued material, the hood of which entirely hid his face. Gerhart could see two red, antler-like horns protruding from holes in the cowl of the cloak and he had a sickening feeling that they weren't simply part of some helm or other head adornment.

The figure held an ivory rod tightly in one brass-gauntleted hand. It was surmounted by a cut black gem, a substance unknown to the fire wizard.

Gerhart spotted something moving at the figure's feet which looked horribly like a hairless human head attached to a pink-fleshed worm-like body.

This was one of the blasphemous warp-mages who had dedicated their lives, their service, their very souls to the immortal gods of disorder and destruction. This was a sorcerer of Chaos and writhing languidly at its feet was his familiar, a creature formed from the very stuff of magic.

The fire mage shivered at the sight. It was all becoming clear to him now.

The warband had no great guns of its own, so the Chaos sorcerer was doubtless intending to use his own devilish powers to turn the artillery piece into some kind of monstrous hell-cannon. Such a transformation demanded a thrice-cursed ritual.

'We have to stop this,' Gerhart hissed to Captain Reimann.

'I agree,' Karl replied quietly, 'but how do you suggest we accomplish such a thing?'

'Your men outnumber the sorcerer's warband.'

'Yes, they do, and they are brave men. I am not one to put down my own men, but one Reiklander halberdier can hardly hope to prevail against a fully-armed and armoured warrior-servant of the Dark Gods.'

'But this ritual must be stopped,' Gerhart growled.

Gerhart was suddenly aware of a guttural chanting coming from the quarry. The words being uttered by the Chaos sorcerer were in a language that no human tongue was ever meant to speak.

As the sorcerer intoned his daemonic incantations, Gerhart could feel the air thickening around him and an uncomfortable pressure building in his ears. He looked down into the quarry with his mage-sight. His eyes began watering, as he saw the throbbing waves of black power emanating from the Chaos sorcerer and the magic-suffused cannon.

And as the sorcerer continued to chant, the Chaos warriors collected blades that had been heated in the white-hot coals of the forge and formed a circle around the cannon.

As the pitch of the sorcerer's corrupt chanting reached a crescendo, the Chaos warriors stepped forward, plunging their glowing blades into the bodies of the men strapped to the cannon. Several jerked into life only to scream a death-agony into the night as their lifeblood poured from their bodies over the cannon.

Steam rose from the men's bodies as the blades cooled in the blood of the victims. Eventually the mist obscured everything from Gerhart's view.

Shaking his head, as if trying to shake himself free of the oppressive feeling pressing down on him, he pushed himself up onto his feet and made to move for the gully leading into the quarry.

'The time for talk is over!' the wizard snarled. 'If you will not act, then I must. Alone, if necessary. Something must be done!'

Then the sky exploded and Gerhart was thrown to the ground.

A CORUSCATING BOLT of jagged crimson lightning tore the sky asunder as it streaked out of the benighted heavens and struck the body of the alchemist who was tied to the top of the cannon. The gold wizard's corpse writhed as the infernal energies drove into it, straining against the heavy iron chains holding it in place.

'Something has been summoned,' said Captain Reimann in his gruff voice. The wizard had picked himself up and was back at the commander's side. 'The gold wizard's glittering soul must have been the

tasty morsel the sorcerer was intending to use to lure a
daemon of Chaos into blasphemous metallurgical creation.' The wizard seemed keen to share his knowledge
with the halberdier.

Karl couldn't tear his eyes from the scene in the
quarry beneath him. In all his years of service as a soldier, he had never witnessed such a horrific event.

Even a man with a resolve as strong as his would
need a moment to compose himself before he could
act. As he gathered his wits, Karl became aware of a
strengthening wind whipping around the hilltop and
the quarry. The blood-daubed cannon and the
writhing corpse bound to it was obscured from view
by billows of filthy black smoke and steam. The wind
continued to rise, tugging at the halberdiers' clothes,
hair and helms as they hugged the ground at the edge
of the quarry cliff.

'What's happening?' Karl shouted over the roar of
the spiralling wind.

'As I said, something has been summoned,' the
bright wizard called back, the gale-force wind whipping his straggly greying hair around his face. 'The
sorcerer has completed his foul begotten ritual. Let us
hope we can still defeat the daemonic spirit he has
brought to this world while it is still vulnerable.'

The wizard staggered to his feet, staff in hand, his
ruddy robes flapping around him.

Karl knew the sorcerer was right.

'Wait!' Karl shouted after the wizard. 'What you need
is a distraction.'

WITH AN APOCALYPTIC boom, the black-powder barrels
exploded on the far side of the quarry. The wagon that
had been holding them was blown apart by the

explosion, sending barrels shooting up into the night sky blazing trails of sparks after them, like giant fireworks. A roiling cloud of fiery smoke rolled across the Chaos encampment.

Shouts went up from the Chaos warriors as they ran to recover their weapons. Gerhart could hear the shrieking of the Chaos sorcerer as he strode into the quarry, through the chaos and confusion. Then he was aware of another sound: the agitated shouts of Captain Reimann's men as they piled into the Chaos camp to engage the enemy.

Gerhart saw two halberdiers cut down one of the black-armoured warriors just as the Chaos-worshipper was pulling a mace from a stand of weapons. One of the men cut his legs from under him. He hooked his halberd in behind the warrior's knees where there was a gap between his armoured greaves, while the second Reiklander thrust his blade up under the gorget of the warrior's breastplate and gutted the foul thing with a twist of the long blade.

The distraction had worked: a couple of scrambling Empire soldiers had entered the camp unseen and made use of a tinderbox, flints and powder barrels that had not yet been put to use.

The fire wizard could have ignited the barrels himself but the evil atmosphere pervading the quarry was making it hard to focus his power. They all had their roles to play. Captain Reimann had made it clear that he and his men would engage the Chaos warriors in combat while Gerhart attempted to reach the hellish machine and use his magic to destroy the daemon-imbued contraption.

The commander of the Reiklanders himself was in the thick of the fighting. Gerhart saw him find his mark in the eye-slit of a warrior's helmet. There was a gargling barking cry and the warrior lurched backwards. Reimann flicked the caught helmet from his opponent's head.

For a moment Gerhart caught sight of the snarling dogface that was exposed beneath. Then he shook the helmet free of his weapon's blade and as the Chaos warrior raised his own jagged-edged broadsword, he thrust forwards again, slicing into the warrior's neck and pushing out the other side. Holding the twitching Chaos-mutant at arm's reach on the end of his halberd, Reimann unsheathed his sword and, stepping forward, brought it up into the Chaos warrior's side, finding an opening in his armour beneath his armpit. The dog-faced mutant crumpled to its knees, gasping its last, blood bubbling from the opening in its throat.

Striding through the choking pall, Gerhart drew the tendrils of Aqshy's crimson energies to him, the candle flame in his mind's eye becoming a raging conflagration. The billowing clouds of spark-shot smoke parted and Gerhart found himself in front of the blasphemous hell-cannon.

The weapon that stood before him was barely recognisable as an Imperial cannon: it had become an appalling amalgam of metal and living flesh. Its long barrel was black iron banded with brass with bonymetal spikes protruding along its length. The muzzle of the great gun now resembled a misshapen, fanged maw and as the wizard watched, a purple whip-like tongue darted from it.

The wheeled gun carriage had been changed by the ritual too. The rear axle and wheels appeared the same, except that now they had spiked teeth around their rims. The front wheels of the carriage had gone, transformed into clawed feet that gripped the ground with scaly, iron talons.

The most horrifying thing about the transformation was what had happened to the poor souls sacrificed to the Chaos powers to bring about the hideous metamorphosis. Little was still visible of the cannon-crew and Eisen Zauber. The men had become fused with the cannon and Gerhart could see their agonised faces screaming from amidst the pulsing, veined metal of the gun's belly. Scalded arms writhed and twisted from the surface of the hell-cannon and clawed at the air.

Gerhart heard a belching rumble from somewhere within the construction and saw the sides of the cannon expand momentarily. What should have been flesh and blood had become armour-skinned and what should have been solid iron had become as living flesh.

The fire wizard knew what he had to do. Somehow, the vile contraption had to be destroyed while the daemonic spirit now imbuing the gun with its warping essence was still exposed. Before he could even get near to the awakening daemon engine, there was the Chaos sorcerer to contend with.

Gerhart saw the sorcerer lower the tip of his ivory staff. The black gem began pulsing malignantly as a twisted spell began to form, but the bright wizard was ready for him. Gerhart had the advantage: the Chaos sorcerer was not expecting the arrival of another wizard into this maelstrom of a Chaos camp.

A cone of fire jetted from the tip of Gerhart's outstretched staff. The furious flames enveloped the antlered sorcerer, and seemed to consume him. Power blazed for several long seconds before the wizard cancelled the conjuration, knowing that he would be in further need of his powers later.

He felt drained after the expenditure of magical energy. The magic had its price and took its toll without regard for the wizard. His cheeks felt drawn and he had a haggard, hollow-eyed look about him now.

There in front of him stood the sorcerer, seemingly unharmed. He shook the last of the dying flames from his cloak as if they were water.

Dispel, Gerhart thought, and let out an angry growl. As his anger built, so did the fiery power burning within him.

The tip of the wizard's staff caught alight with an audible *whoomph*. Holding the oak rod in his right hand like a javelin, Gerhart drew his arm back and hurled it forward with all his might. The blazing staff soared from his hand, trailing fire, until it found its mark. The sorcerer screamed as the burning brand struck him full in the face, and remained there. The cowl of the sorcerer's robe burst into flame and soon his whole head was wreathed in fire. The screams died and the sorcerer toppled forwards, tumbling from the rock onto the ground and remained there, motionless.

Gerhart recovered his staff and turned its still blazing tip on the monstrous contraption before him. Sheets of flame poured from the smouldering oak, dousing the cannon in hot, purifying fire. But against the hellish contraption Gerhart's fiery spell seemed to have little effect. The cannon had been forged in fires hotter than this and to the daemon now possessing the machine, fire was of no consequence at all. The fires of hell were hotter, after all.

Gerhart was suddenly aware of a hissing sound close to his feet and felt something brush against his leg. He looked down to see the slithering pink coils of the sorcerer's familiar wrapping around his leg. He lashed out just as the hairless, human head opened distended snake-like jaws and sank inch-long fangs into his calf. Shaken free, the familiar landed in the hot coals of a glowing bonfire. There it died, shrivelling to nothing more than a fire-blackened husk.

The bite stung, but it did not feel as if any noxious poison had been injected into his bloodstream, for which Gerhart was profoundly grateful. With the familiar dealt with, the bright wizard turned his attention back to the hell-cannon.

There was a throaty belching sound and a flame-wreathed cannonball blasted from the fanged maw of the gun. Clouds of putrid black smoke emitted from oil-dripping orifices at the rear of the contraption. Gerhart inhaled a great lungful of the reeking emission and began coughing violently. His eyes began streaming again.

Blinking away the tears, Gerhart saw the ruin of a Reiklander lying beside the wreckage of a wagon. His bones were broken and his body had been blasted open by the deadly cannonball that was now embedded in the wall of the quarry. There was a second belching boom and the gun fired at another corner where the Imperial soldiers were still holding back the Chaos warriors. The machine had hauled itself around to locate a fresh target.

Gerhart had not even known the cannon had been loaded, and now he wondered whether it was creating its own ammunition from within. It had to be stopped!

He ran forward, drawing the tempered steel of his sword. He dropped his precious staff so that he could hold the blade firmly in both hands. The fire mage was not a confident swordsman. Gerhart thought he could see a crack in the bulging side of the cannon. It was a possible vulnerable spot, a weak point in its construction. He swung his sword in a mighty arc at the engine. The blade struck the spot and, to Gerhart's dismay, shattered. Casting the useless hilt of the weapon aside he closed his eyes and reached into his mind.

There, in the dark void, the fire of his wizardly power blazed, only now the flames tapered and twisted as they burned, taking on a new form; something like a sword.

Gerhart opened his eyes. There in his hands was a sword of flame. The mystical weapon warmed the palms of his hands but did not burn the fire mage. He prepared to swing this conjured fiery blade at the same point of apparent weakness on the wheezing cannon.

Then it hit him.

It was like a wave of sickening nausea only it was backed by a sinister sentience of its own. Suddenly all Gerhart could focus on was the blood pumping from the cannon and the writhing of its perverted metal-flesh limbs. Whatever it was that resided in the warped weapon would not have the wizard thwart it so easily.

Gerhart could feel the bile rising in his throat as steel-tipped claws scraped at the inside of his skull. He felt overwhelmed. The sights, sounds and smells of the battle raging all around him ruined his concentration even more. The cries of the Reiklanders as they fell to Chaos blades. The obscene monstrosity that was the hell-cannon filling his field of vision. The smell of the smoke and the crackling of flames.

Flames.

Fire.

The whirling wind of Aqshy. The very essence of his power.

With an almighty bodily effort and a roar born of anger, pain and desperate fear, the bright wizard swung the blazing blade.

As the flame-wreathed sword hit the groaning metal body of the daemon engine, its tip pierced the machine's iron hide. Human hands emerged from the metal barrel, and clutched at the wizard. It seemed as if the blade was cutting into hot, pumping flesh and blood. The body of the gun-engine swelled and Gerhart forced the fiery sword in still further, twisting it with all his strength – physical and magical.

An agonised squeal howled from the muzzle of the hell-cannon and the hands emerging from its sides became palsied clenching claws. Gerhart had a fair idea what would happen next. He pulled the magical weapon from the belly of the daemonic cannon and ran, the flaming blade evaporating into ether.

The explosion drowned out the cacophony of battle raging in the quarry, and the force of it threw halberdiers and Chaos warriors flat. The daemon bound within the cannon was being thrown back to the Realm of Chaos that had spawned it – the hellish alchemical construction could no longer contain the writhing, warping energies. Chunks of smouldering, twisted metal and gobbets of half-cooked meat rained down across the encampment. Red smoke washed across the floor of the quarry like a bloody fog.

Gerhart picked himself up – as did the survivors of Captain Reimann's halberdiers and the last of the Chaos warband. His ears rang with the deafening roar of the daemon engine's apocalyptic demise.

Now they knew the fate of the cannon-team, the only thing Gerhart's party could do was return to Wolfenburg, with all due haste, and report what they had discovered. Disturbingly, however, they still were none the wiser as to what had become of the knights.

Even with the Chaos sorcerer dead and the daemon engine destroyed, the wizard could still sense the power of Chaos pulsing beneath the surface of reality. The coming storm of Chaos would almost be at the gates of ancient Wolfenburg and the fire mage could do nothing to thwart it here.

First, the survivors of the daemon-loving warband had to be made to atone for their hellish sins. Staff back in hand, its tip aflame once more, Gerhart charged into the fray, cursing the Chaos warriors with every oath he knew. And the wrath of a wizard of the Bright order was terrible indeed.

TEN
The Whim of the Dark Gods

*'Our pitiful lives are governed by nothing more
than the uncaring seasons and the whim
of the Dark Gods.'*

– From the writings of
Mandrus the Heretic

'SO HERE WE are again, Vendhal Skullwarper,' the high
zar said, his voice imbued with a tone of annoyance.

'Yes, lord seh,' the Chaos sorcerer said, casting his
eyes away from the hideous visage of the lord of the
Kurgan horde.

Surtha Lenk had summoned Vendhal to his
appalling pavilion at dawn. He knew why. There was
dissent among the ranks. The zars and their warbands were hungry for blood and victory and after
the ease with which they had taken Aachden they

were becoming frustrated. They were looking for someone to blame for the stalemate, and many accused Surtha Lenk for bringing them to this impasse.

The sorcerer had approached the tent, pitched behind the ranked mass of the Kurgan, with trepidation. It was as blasphemous and corrupted a creation as the warlord of the Northmen host himself. The fabric of the pavilion was composed of tanned human skin, the guy ropes were of plaited sinew, its support poles made from calcified spines. As Vendhal had passed through the breeze-batted flaps of the entrance, the familiar stench of decay and cloying perfume washed over him.

It was dark inside the battle tent. An acrid fog of incense palled from hanging brass lamps so that the sorcerer could not see the floor. He was aware of a dull susurrating sound, however, like dry, serpentine coils twisting and writhing over the floor of the tent.

'Here we are again, and still Wolfenburg remains to be broken. I am... displeased, Vendhal Skullwarper,' the high zar burbled.

The sorcerer said nothing. Things brushed against his cloak in the dark, their touch like feathers, their voices an inhuman chittering.

'Why have you not yet used your prestigious sorcerous powers to break the siege?'

Surtha Lenk was looking for someone to blame too and he had singled out the sorcerer chief.

'As I have told you, lord seh, we are far from the Shadow of the north and its influence.'

'You would lecture me?' the high zar snarled. 'Is it not true that where we march under the banners of Lord Tzeen, the influence of the Shadow also grows? The world changes as we pass.'

'That is true, lord seh,' the sorcerer conceded. 'But with the sun high in the sky for so much of the day, the Eye of Tzeen cannot suffer its glare. So it remains closed for most of the time.'

'Then the sun must not be permitted to blind Lord Tzeen any longer. See to it, Vendhal Skullwarper, or your soul will be given up in sacrifice to the greatest of sorcerers.'

The Chaos sorcerer took a deep breath. He still could not look directly at the crimson armoured giant and the grotesque swaddling babe harnessed to its front.

'My powers have been weakened by this environment,' the sorcerer explained angrily, admitting to the truth of the situation. 'If I am to gather the power needed, lord seh, an atrocity on a grand scale will be needed...'

'If that is what it will take,' Surtha Lenk said, his voice giggling once again at the prospect of greater slaughter in the name of Chaos, 'then that is what must happen.'

'Yes, lord seh,' Vendhal said, bowing. He had not once cast his eyes on the warlord. He retreated from Surtha Lenk's presence, and backed out of the tent.

'Oh, one other thing, sorcerer,' Lenk said in his squeaking, high-pitched voice, just as Vendhal reached the entrance of the tent. 'If you continue to... displease me, I shall gut you myself and tear your soul from your dying body.'

THE BIG PUSH came the following day, as dusk was spreading its twilight veil over Ostland. That night warriors from every warband under Surtha Lenk's banner assaulted the walls of Wolfenburg, and the

Northmen's war machines renewed their meteoric missile attacks on the sentinel city, hurling death at its ancient walls.

At first, the city's siege defences and garrison held off the attacks, but as the night wore on past the second watch, the size of the attack increased. So great were the numbers of barbarians assaulting the walls, that the bodies of the Northmen lay ten deep at its foot. These mounds of the dead provided other battle-maddened marauders means to clamber further up the ramparts and attack the city's defenders.

There was nothing the Imperial defenders could do but ride out and meet the Northmen's attack. Fully half the standing army of Wolfenburg, the knights of the Order of the Silver Mountain and a hastily conscripted town militia charged out of the gates of the city as the great doors opened.

There was worse to come for the noble champions of the city.

As soon as the brave defenders left the relative security of their bastion, the Chaos horde turned from the walls, leaving their dead behind them without a second thought, to face Wolfenburg's guardians. Those left inside the city had no choice but to close and bar the gates behind the overwhelmed soldiers: they could not risk losing all and allowing the Northmen into Wolfenburg. But, to their credit, not one of the brave Imperial defenders, even those drawn from the city militia, ever attempted to re-enter the city. Against such overwhelming odds, however, there was nothing the Imperial troops could do.

That night, Surtha Lenk's horde captured more living prisoners than they had done so far. The defenders of Wolfenburg watched from the walls as their fellow men were dragged to the Kurgan encampments. What troubled them was that the Northmen had taken virtually no prisoners until this point. What could they possibly have in mind for the poor wretches they now took? Why did they need so many living souls?

The wall guards and their commanders crossed themselves with the sign of the holy hammer but dared think no more upon their damned brethren. There was no helping them now. They were already as good as dead – or worse.

Amongst the Kurgan there was a great deal of celebration and carousing. Many of the marauders, frustrated by weeks of inaction, felt that at last something was being done to break the city. Hope filled their hearts once more. They were elated to have taken so many prisoners.

Hope also came with the rumour that a lone warrior among the warbands of the high zar's army had been singled out by the power known to those wild men as Tchar or Tzeen. He had brought the luck of that unholy deity to Surtha Lenk's enterprise.

A time of great change was coming, all could feel it – loyal servants of the Empire and sons of the north alike.

BRUISED AND BATTERED, Lector Wilhelm Faustus was dumped unceremoniously on the leaf-littered floor of the clearing between the gnarled and twisted oak trees. Groans came from around him as survivors of his party who had also pursued the fleeing war herd into the Forest of Shadows were dropped next to him.

The beastmen had taken them all by surprise from the cover of the trees. It was easy once they strayed too far into the green-shot twilight of the forest – and so

the men when they became separated from one
another. Wilhelm had come round to find himself tied
to a broken tree branch slung between two of the
beastmen. Another of the creatures carried his heavy
warhammer over its shoulder.

The group made fast progress through the forest.
The pack that had captured the priest had soon joined
up with others who had captured more of Wilhelm's
entourage. He didn't know what had become of his
loyal steed Kreuz.

They had been carried through the Forest of Shadows, strung from denuded branches, with the hot stink
of the beastmen reeking in their nostrils, and the
sounds of grunts and guttural barks ringing in their
ears. The tongue of the beastmen was as unintelligible
as the lowing of cattle or the bleating of sheep.

They had been travelling for a day, the priest judged,
deeper and deeper into the dark and untamed woodland. The trees grew closely here, but they were dark
and twisted parodies of natural life. The beastmen
waded through briar thickets, brambles and nettle
beds without a second thought: their tough animal
hides protected them. The Sigmarites were not so for-
tunate, however. By comparison their skin was as soft
as a Bretonnian damsel's. Wilhelm felt every scratch
and sting as thorns dug into his flesh and prickly net-
tles brushed his face and the exposed skin of his arms.

The beastmen had not done anything to remove his
armour, even though they had taken his holy weapon.
The additional weight didn't trouble them at all. They
were lean, hard-muscled creatures, thanks to their
tribal existence.

And so, after an unpleasantly uncomfortable journey, the lector and his followers now found

themselves at the very heart of the beastmen's territory, inside the creatures' camp.

The beasts' prisoners were released from the poles, either by cutting the twine that bound them or by simply biting through the knots with their sharp teeth. The ungors, directed by their larger, whip-wielding cousins, poked and prodded at the humans with rough spears until they had goaded them into a crude cage in the clearing. It was constructed from tree branches, tied together with more twine and dried animal gut, in a haphazard fashion. But the cage served its purpose. Once all of the men had been hustled inside a heavy log was pushed through two loops of rope to keep the door shut. It wasn't the most complicated of locks but it too served its purpose. With a whole herd of beastmen squatting only a few feet away, escape was improbable, in fact impossible.

But for Wilhelm Faustus, a faithful servant of Sigmar, there was no such thing as impossible as long as he maintained his faith in the Heldenhammer. And never was the light of Sigmar needed more than in this forsaken forest, dedicated to darker, fell powers.

Everything about the beastman camp stank like a midden. The cage reeked of filth and rotting meat, the lingering odour of its last unfortunate occupants no doubt. The priest could smell a dung heap nearby, and everywhere was the all-pervasive musky smell of the herd.

Wilhelm noticed that the hugely muscled red-furred beastman, which had led the whole expedition, was now exerting its authority over the others. Its red hide set it apart from the rest, and no doubt meant that it had been singled out for greatness by the Dark Gods they worshipped. Amongst the beastmen might was most definitely right, the strong dominating the weak. Life amongst the herd was a case of the survival of the fittest.

There were other beastmen here too. They seemed, to the ever-observant priest, to be arranged into small warbands, as if they formed the units of the larger, combined war herd.

Trapped inside the stinking cage, Wilhelm took a moment to study the layout of the camp. The clearing was roughly half a mile long and a quarter of a mile across, surrounded on all sides by dense forest. Wilhelm had been aware that the ground had been rising steadily since that morning, but now that he was in the clearing it was more obvious that they were on higher ground. Craggy granite teeth broke from the turf and dirt of the clearing and Wilhelm could see no higher outcrops of land beyond the tops of the trees.

The beastmen had made their camp next to a crude stone circle that stood within the clearing, close to its northern edge. At the centre of the circle of weather-worn monoliths was a single stone, twice as tall as the others, that looked like it had dropped from the heavens and had landed upright. Wilhelm could only guess at who, or even what, had raised these granite menhirs. He could feel that their purpose was not worthy. The psychically sensitive holy man could sense a great evil hanging over the camp, like some malign entity hungry for the souls of mortal men. The towering stone, in whose shadow they lay, seemed to pulse with its own malign power.

Adorning the stone were the corpses of several armoured knights, They were hanging from gore-encrusted chains and great butcher's hooks, and they had been horribly disfigured by the injuries they had suffered. Several were missing limbs, others looked like they had been partially devoured and one had been disembowelled: the warrior's viscera were strung out over the rock along with the chains. All of the dismembered cadavers were caked in dried blood, obscuring their features. It looked as if the knights' tabards might once have been white. Various scratch-like runes and sigils had been daubed on the surface of the monolith in blood, but Wilhelm could not look at them for long because they made his eyes water and he could feel a headache forming behind his eyes.

Dumped at the base of the huge standing stone were the herd's many trophies taken in battle and raids on the peoples whose dwellings bordered the Forest of Shadows. There was everything from weapons and armour of the herd's bested foes to skulls, human and otherwise, and battle banners. Some of them looked very old and were almost nothing more than torn, mildewed rags.

One of the banners, although its design was antique, looked like it had been in a fairly good state of repair before the beastmen had got their filthy paws on it. It was bloodstained and soiled with mud and faeces like the rest of the captured standards. Wilhelm couldn't help thinking that there was something familiar about the crest the banner bore.

As Wilhelm watched, a gor wrested his holy warhammer from the ungor that had been carrying it and tossed it onto the mound of prizes. The weapons that had been taken from the other members of Wilhelm's captured party were also added to the collection to gather rust.

'I know that standard,' a voice whispered hotly in Wilhelm's ear.

He looked round. A balding, grey-haired swords-man who had joined his following at Haracre was standing there looking towards the tribe's herdstone with a mixture of appalled horror and nervous excite-ment. The warrior priest knew which standard he meant.

'How come?' Wilhelm asked.

'I once fought under that very banner,' the man said. He was one of the few amongst Wilhelm's zealous Sig-marite band who had ever been a professional soldier. 'In my youth. When I stood with the standing army of the Elector Count of Ostland to purge the farmlands south of Kosterun of a greenskin incursion. It is the battle banner of the ancient sentinel city of the north. It is the Wolfenburg standard!'

'The Wolfenburg standard you say?' Wilhelm repeated, half to himself.

'Yes, your holiness.'

'Then that ancient city is, as we suspected, in the direst danger.' Wilhelm knew the legends: that should the city be assaulted whilst lacking the presence of the ancient war banner, then it would surely fall. 'We must recover that standard and return it to its rightful home,' he said, his purpose clear.

'What will become of us?' a cowering forester asked, his right eye swollen and bruised from the treatment he had suffered at the hands of the beastly ambushers.

'Is it not as plain as the nose on your face?' a rag-robed flagellant snapped. 'We are to be sacrificed to the beast-things' foul gods! Why else have they kept us alive and brought us all the way here? Is that not right?' the flagellant asked, turning to Wilhelm.

'When the time is right,' the warrior priest rumbled.

'Perhaps when the correct constellations are visible in the sky overhead,' another, much older priest suggested.

'And what do we do until then?' the forester persisted, gloomily.

'We keep our faith in Sigmar, and wait,' the warrior priest said.

This was not the death – the martyrdom – he sought. Lector Wilhelm Faustus still had much work to do. He would not wait to be made a sacrifice to the foul gods that lived beyond the veil of reality. Now he had a new purpose. He not only had to escape from the clutches of these children of Chaos but he and his men had an obligation to recover the Wolfenburg standard and return it to the ancient city.

Wilhelm returned to watching the beastmen, on the lookout for an opportunity when he and his men could act against their captors and exact their revenge at last.

IT WAS SEVERAL days later that Wilhelm was presented with the opportunity he had been patiently waiting for. He had been watching the beastmen constantly, and studying the arrangement of the herd and its hierarchical pecking order.

Unsurprisingly, the conditions inside the cramped cage were rapidly worsening. Now the imprisoned entourage smelt as strongly of their own waste as they did of the permeating reek of the beastmen. Their captors had fed them scraps of raw meat. The captives couldn't be allowed to die before they were to be sacrificed, after all. The priest had readily wolfed down whatever had been thrown his way. He needed to keep his strength up.

Dawn broke cold and damp even though it was a summer's day. As the warrior priest woke amidst the filth and detritus littering the cage floor, he felt his body aching as it did every morning thanks to the rough, uneven surface. A hubbub of noise permeated the camp and it soon became clear why.

A troupe that Wilhelm had not seen before had entered the clearing. At first the priest wondered if they were members of a rival warband, come to claim the campsite as their own, but it soon became apparent that they were an accepted part of the tribe. The small force of beastmen was led by a monstrous creature, unlike the others in shape or form. It, and the three warped creatures of its retinue, were bull-headed monstrosities, nearly twice the height of a man and far greater in bulk, but the leader was by far the largest.

The minotaur, obviously a champion among its kind, was a huge, pot-bellied creature, with arms of bulging corded muscle. Its ugly, broad, snouted head was surrounded by a dark, shaggy mane. The distance from one sharpened horn tip to the other was somewhere around two spans Wilhelm supposed. Around its neck, the minotaur wore a spiked collar. It had little else in the way of armour, but spiked, curved steel plates protected its shoulders. A studded harness crossed its chest and at the centre of this was a bronze disc inscribed with the eight-pointed star of Chaos. The jutting-jawed head of an orc hung from the belt of its loincloth and it carried two heavy axes – one in each of its massive man-like hands. One of the weapons looked like it might have been dwarfish, before the intricate etchings on its blade had been defaced and inscribed by altogether more malignant markings.

The minotaur was a creature to inspire awe and dread in both its allies and enemies alike. It was a doombull, as the champions of bull-men were known.

The minotaur's warband was dragging a roughly-constructed sled weighed down with yet more battle trophies, but they did not appear to be human in origin. The party had obviously returned from its own raiding expedition and, as far as Wilhelm could tell from the brutal looking artefacts, it had been against the greenskins.

Up until that moment, Wilhelm had considered that they had seen all of the beast-tribe. But now it was clear that the force his entourage had faced at Walderand was only part of the war herd.

The lector observed the reactions of the rest of the warherd to the doombull's arrival. Beastmen scurried out of the minotaur's way, gors lowered their heads an inch and some of the ungors even urinated or defecated, in deference to their leader.

But not all of the herd behaved in this way. As the doombull approached the stone circle, Wilhelm could see the red-skinned bestigor and his followers were making no reverences before the bull-headed monster.

To begin with it seemed that the minotaur was totally unaware of this or that it ignored it in its feral arrogance. The rest of the doombull's party added the arms and armour they had taken from the greenskins to the rusting and foetid pile at the foot of the great standing stone. It was only when this was done that the monstrous minotaur turned its attention towards the unabashed wargor.

Raising both axes in the air the minotaur snorted and bellowed at the bestigor, its bull eyes blazing. In response, the red-skinned wargor raised its own cleaver-like falchion in both clawed hands and, throwing back its head, with an ululating cry, howled its challenge to the sky.

The scene unfolding before them transfixed all in the camp – men and beastmen. Wilhelm doubted that any of his fellow prisoners fully understood what was going on. The warrior priest, however, had studied various permitted texts concerning the enemies of Sigmar's light, and their practices. He could guess what was going on. The rebellious wargor was making its challenge for the position of sire of the tribe. The wargor had captured a great prize: souls to be sacrificed to the herd's animalistic gods. It believed itself worthy of the title of Banebeast.

Then there was nothing more to be said.

The minotaur and the wargor, traded blow after blow against each other. They fought with the ferocity of rabid dogs, grunting, snarling and bellowing at one another as they did so. At first they seemed evenly matched, in terms of size, strength and animal cunning. As the doombull's dwarf axe cut down towards the wargor's neck, the bestigor parried with a strike of its falchion. As the red-skinned challenger thrust with its own blade, the minotaur caught the knocked edge with the hook of its Chaos-forged war-axe. The two beasts also tried to kick and bite and gore one another. Nothing was too base for these degenerate creatures.

Then suddenly, twisting its great bulk out of the way of the wargor's descending falchion-blade, the minotaur skewered its challenger's shoulder with one of its sharpened horn tips. The doombull had demonstrated why it was the leader of the tribe. With great muscles in its bull neck bulging, the minotaur lifted the other beastman off the ground, impaled on the end of its horn.

As the wargor kicked out at the minotaur's loins with its sharp-hoofed feet, the herd-leader brought both of its axes around in front of its body, delivering two savage cuts that sliced open the gor's stomach. The red-skinned beastman gave a shrieking cry as its entrails burst from the ruptured flesh in a torrent of black blood and offal. The doombull shook the beastman free of its horn and the challenger fell to the ground, wailing like a newborn calf.

But the doombull did not stop. The frenzy of bloodgreed was on it now. The leader threw itself on the dying, gutted challenger and took a great bite out of its laboured heaving chest. The doombull threw back its head, blood dripping from its chin, and gulped down the bloody lump of gouged meat.

Having witnessed such savage brutality, bloodlust had taken hold of the tribe. The scent of blood was in their nostrils, and blood was pumping in their veins. Blood was the only thing that would satisfy them now!

The beastmen were not quelled by the death of the wargor; they were giddy with the scent of carnage and wanted nothing more than to have their bestial cravings sated in battle. They divided into two camps – those who wished to avenge the upstart that slayed their wargor, and the others loyal to the doombull.

The two sides immediately clashed in the middle of the clearing. With the prisoners forgotten, beastman fought beastman in an orgy of bloodletting. As some of Wilhelm's followers watched the confusion of the battle, wary of any stray axes or battling combatants coming their way, the warrior priest and the stronger soldiers began to wrestle the heavy log-bolt that held the cage shut. They struggled to free the securing ropes, all the while straining to reach it through the haphazard bars.

One of the men gave a cry as he saw something hurtling towards the prisoners. With a crash, a hulking gor smashed into the side of the cage and through the splintered bars. As the injured beastman struggled to rise, Wilhelm grabbed a splintered stake and plunged it through the soft flesh of the creature's neck. The gor died choking on its own foul blood.

Chaos reigned in the clearing. The cries of the battling beastmen echoed around the stone pillars of the lithic circle. Metal rang on metal and stone. But Wilhelm Faustus and his Sigmarite crusaders were free.

'We have no time to lose,' the priest told his men. 'We must recover our weapons and leave this place.'

None of the priest's followers disputed this decision. They were weak after days of imprisonment and knew that they were hopelessly outnumbered by the beastmen. Luckily the herd was doing more harm to itself than Wilhelm's holy entourage could ever hope to.

For that was Chaos's greatest weakness, the lector knew. It would always turn on itself and destroy itself, in the end.

It must have taken a terrifyingly powerful individual to unite the northern hordes to attack the Empire with a common purpose. And they were backed by all four of the fell Chaos powers.

Wilhelm ducked and weaved through the melee, avoiding sweeping war-axes, crushing hooves and goring horns as he made for the great, central standing stone. The most confident of his followers followed him. Angry battling beastmen hurtled past them, grappling with one another. To some, such action might seem like madness. But as a warrior priest of Sigmar there was no other option, how could he abandon his consecrated weapon? A lector of Sigmar was nothing without his holy warhammer, the tool with which he delivered the God-Emperor's justice.

A beastman with its flesh bearing tattooed whorls and spirals suddenly turned towards Wilhelm and snarled. It was bowled over as another gor, its hide the same colour as the minotaur's challenger, slammed into it, curved ram's horns butting it in the stomach. Wilhelm darted past the outer edge of the stone circle and in three long strides reached the treasure pile. A moment later his warhammer was in his hands. Gripping its haft tightly between his gauntleted hands, he felt the righteous power of Sigmar surge through his body.

There was a crash and bellowing close behind him. He turned, warhammer ready. The almost-deposed doombull was suddenly on top of Wilhelm, its animal breath gusting in his face. He became wet with saliva and mucus. An ungor was hanging from one of the minotaur's great, outstretched arms by its teeth. The minotaur tried to shake it free, at the same time trying to extricate a dwarf axe from the carcass of a boar-headed beastman in his other hand. Despite such encumbrances, the minotaur still tried to snap at the priest with blunt teeth, darkly malevolent fire burning in its eyes.

In the presence of the cruel beast, the head of Wilhelm's recovered warhammer burst into golden flame. Reacting instinctively, heart pounding, Wilhelm brought the weapon round in a great arc, slamming the blunt head of the hammer down on top of the minotaur's unprotected skull.

There was a crack like a thunderclap and the great, tough cranium fractured. The doombull bellowed in surprise and pain and reeled, throwing the ungor from its arm and tugging the dwarf axe free in the same lunging spasm. Before it could focus through the fog of concussion Wilhelm had struck again, this time landing the head of the hammer squarely against the side of the monster's head. The doombull's face collapsed, splintering inwards. Shards of thickened bone carved through the pulped grey matter beneath, which in turn spurted from other cracks in the minotaur's shattered skull.

Toppling like a great, lightning-struck oak, the minotaur crashed to the ground. Its tongue flopped from its slack mouth and slapped against the warrior priest's booted feet. The doombull, once so favoured by its Dark Gods, had clearly lost that favour now, and with it its ill-begotten life.

With the monstrous minotaur defeated, the rest of Wilhelm's party rushed to collect their weapons from the pile at the bottom of the defaced herdstone. Wilhelm took hold of the ancient Wolfenburg banner and led the escape from the odious camp.

Armed once again, and with the beastmen preoccupied with the battle raging in the clearing, it did not take the Sigmarites long to fight their way clear of the tumult, running for the fringes of the forest and the cover the trees provided. The forest closed around them again and the bellows, hoots and braying cries of the beastmen dwindled into the distance.

Wilhelm and his band had regained their freedom. Whether it was thanks to the benediction of Sigmar, as the priest liked to believe, or simply the vagaries of fate, or even the whim of Dark Gods, Lector Wilhelm

Faustus and his band had escaped the fate the beast-men had intended for them.

It had been Sigmar's will all along, the warrior priest believed, that he and his men be taken to the beastmen's camp and recover the Wolfenburg Standard. For the return of the ancient battle banner might very well be the only thing that could turn the tide of the siege in the sentinel city's favour – as long as Wilhelm's party could reach it in time.

ELEVEN
The Eye of the Storm

'The powers of the pyromancer are truly formidable, and where they bend their powers ruin and destruction is sure to follow, no matter what is intended.'

– From *A Treatise of the Lores of Magic*
by Theodoric Wurstein

WOLFENBURG.

It stood before the gathered Chaos horde as a symbol of Imperial might they had to overcome. If it could be conquered, then the whole of Ostland would be Surtha Lenk's for the taking and the Empire would be Archaon's.

As summer began to wane, so the shadow cast by the fluctuating Realm of Chaos broadened, engulfing more of the lands of men. The Chaos host felt its power surging through their bodies, pulsing in their veins with every beat of their hearts. Now in the fourth month of the siege, a host as large as the one that had attacked on the night when the prisoners had been taken was readying itself for the final assault on Wolfenburg.

Drums beat a tattoo of death that was interrupted by the unearthly blaring of carynx horns and the clashing of weapons against armour and shields. In front of the Northmen stood the prisoners they had taken from amongst the valiant defenders of the resilient city. They had been lashed to barbaric symbols constructed from an amalgam of rotten wood, huge bones and rusted metal. They were in the shadow of the horde's leviathan siege engines.

Some of the Northmen's prisoners remained proud and resolute, showing no fear, despite the despicable treatment they had suffered at the hands of the barbarians. Others, however, were whimpering shells of the men they had once been, who screamed their pleas for mercy to the uncaring heavens; they were broken by the atrocities they had suffered and been forced to witness in the daemon-worshippers' camp. Some were no longer aware of what was happening to them; they were either unconscious or their wits had left them, so terrible had been the experience.

The Northmen knew that those watching from the walls of Wolfenburg would be able to see the prisoners and would understand what fate was about to deal them.

Dark clouds were building on the horizon over the Middle Mountains, rolling down from the north to smother the marches of Ostland as they had done during the spring of that year. The wind was picking up too.

Behind the lines formed by the Chaos warbands, Vendhal Skullwarper sat cross-legged within the outline of another blasphemous symbol that had been burnt into the turf of the ground. To any that could bear to look at it, they would see the sigil was that of an eight-pointed star, four spans across which merged with a curving, fish-like form set within a corrupted circle. Where the sigil had been formed, the grass hissed and smouldered, and an acrid smoke rose from the ground where the corrupting influence of Chaos had taken hold.

Other esoteric markings had been made at the various points of these images as well. Around the outside of the ring nine stakes had been thrust into the ground at regular intervals, each topped with a skull, which had been doused in tar and set alight. Despite the wind, these death's-head torches burned brightly.

Vendhal Skullwarper studied the roiling currents of flickering colour that wound and bucked around, above and within his circle of power. He breathed in deeply. The wind brought the smell of death and decay to him as well as the scent of future possibilities. The time was almost ripe. He could feel the strength of the Shadow in his bones; he could see it creeping over the Northlands towards this place, towards the moment when all future possibilities would end. It would grow like a malignant cancer that would ultimately envelop the whole world.

'It is time,' the sorcerer said, his voice heavy with the doom of what was coming to Wolfenburg.

At his word one of the high zar's battle-shamans, wearing nothing but the skin and horns of a stag and wildly applied body paint, capered from where he waited into the ranks of the amassed warbands. He fidgeted nervously.

'It is time.'

'It's time.'

'The time has come.'

'It is time.'

The sorcerer's decree spread through the ranks of the Northmen like wildfire. Then, unnervingly, all the noises ceased. For several seconds, the only sounds were from the mewling and groaning prisoners. Prayers could be heard alongside babbled nonsense, as men commended their souls to Sigmar and others whimpered their agonies to the unheeding air.

Warriors stepped forward from each of the gathered warbands, blades drawn. The marauders held their swords ready. A large, hunchbacked creature raised a brass horn, its trumpet mouth a boar's head, and blew one sonorous note that echoed mournfully over the ground between the two opposing forces. Almost as one man, the chosen warriors raised their swords and axes and executed the prisoners. So much blood washed over the hateful symbols to which the men had been tied that the tinny stink of the life-giving fluid was carried on the breeze to the city itself.

The blood-letting drove the impatient horde into a frenzy. Only the total destruction of their enemy would satisfy them now.

The ritual slaughter of the captured knights and men-at-arms would have as much of an effect on the morale of the city's appalled defenders as it would against Wolfenburg's defences. Now that ritual could begin in earnest.

The sorcerer could feel the forces he needed gathering in the ether around him, drawn by the spilling of blood and the markings of power. He was bound by ancient covenants and summoned by primal emotions. It felt as if he was at the very centre of the roiling storm of magical energy.

The sorcerer could feel the insidious creep of Chaos in every part of his body until it was the realm that existed beyond reality that seemed most real to him. Reality became nothing but a ghostly echo.

The pounding of hooves, the jangle of harnesses and the snorting of horses brought him back to the real world briefly. Twenty riders stood beyond the limit of the magical sigils. Their intrusion irritated the sorcerer but their arrival was necessary for the completion of the ritual Vendhal had begun. They needed to bring the wrath of the Dark Gods down upon the bricks and mortar of Wolfenburg.

The riders were all from the high zar's personal bodyguard. A giant of a man led them who had bullhorns sprouting obscenely from his malformed skull. The big man dismounted and stopped at the edge of the circle.

'You have it?' Vendhal asked.

'I have it,' the bodyguard replied.

'And it has been blessed by the chosen one from amongst Zar Uldin's band?'

'It has.'

'Then give it to me,' the sorcerer commanded.

The horned giant tossed something cold, hard and round into the circle. Vendhal caught it deftly and looked at it. It was a human skull that had been polished to a pearlescent finish. The sorcerer caught the shimmer of rainbow colours skitter over the shiny smooth bone as he turned it in his hand. It had indeed been blessed by the touch of Tchar. Tzeen was looking down upon their enterprise with favour.

Vendhal now had the last piece of the puzzle in his hands. It might only be a human skull, but to one who knew the origin of that skull and the power that it had been imbued with, one also understood that there was no greater instrument of war.

And so Vendhal Skullwarper commenced his dark ritual. The Chaos sigil began to glow and the grass burned black.

The city would fall to the barbarian legions of the high zar and it would fall tonight.

GERHART BRENNEND LOOKED across the bend in the river at the hill rising up to the city beyond. A biting wind blew around him, whipping his robes against his lean, wiry form. He stood firm, however, staff in hand. This rising wind, he knew, was not wholly of natural origin. The tormented weather reflected the turmoil that had seized the flow of the winds of magic sweeping from the north in the wake of the Chaos incursion.

Gerhart could see disturbance all around him. Tendrils of translucent colour whipped overhead or soared from the roiling sky to coil around him in knots and spirals of coruscating, multi-hued energy. Shades of sparkling azure, fiery crimson, burnished gold, glittering emerald, dazzling acid-white, deep purple, dusky grey and earthy umber swept and gusted around him. It was as if a tempest had beset the winds of magic and the more disruption there was within the flow of magical energy, the stronger the effect on the surrounding atmosphere growing over Wolfenburg.

As the hurricane whipped the strands of power around him, Gerhart could also see the tendrils being drawn towards the seething black clouds above the sentinel city. Its great, grey walls now seemed almost black as the day darkened to night. It was as if the glowering thunderheads were drawing the magical energies towards themselves for some fell reason.

This was no midsummer thunderstorm, this was an unseasonable gale that was growing to almost cyclonic proportions. It was as if summer itself were dying. So mighty was the Chaos invasion, and so great the destruction it had caused – whole armies massacred and entire towns laid waste – that the natural world itself seemed to have suffered a mortal wound.

Gerhart and Captain Reimann's regiment stood watching all this from amongst the stand of trees at the top of the hill. Below them was the cave that led to the secret tunnel and the dungeons of Wolfenburg Castle.

They had reached the city in time to see the Kurgan quitting their camps and preparing to bring down Wolfenburg at last. Gerhart knew that they were going to have to get back inside the city. One of Reimann's men had scouted ahead, crawling through the mud and filth of the tunnel again, only to find it blocked after less than half a mile. Just as Gerhart had predicted, once they had escaped the city, those left behind had brought the roof down – with Auswald Strauch's blessing, no doubt.

'We are too late, there is no way back into the city and the attack has already begun,' one of the Reiklanders said dejectedly.

'We are not too late,' the captain chided. 'We can still make a difference.'

'But there are only ten of us left,' another weary soldier pointed out. The halberdiers had paid highly for the destruction of the daemon engine and the antlered sorcerer's warband.

'It does not matter!' Gerhart said, unable to believe what he was hearing. 'While we still breathe we can fight. And while we can still fight we can exact a high toll from those who would bring doom to our ancient city.'

'We are tired, exhausted!' another complained bitterly.

'Enough!' the veteran captain exclaimed. 'Rest while you can, all of you,' he said and many of the halberdiers gratefully sat down on the stones and turf of the hill. 'But be ready to move at my command. Wizard, might I have a word?'

Gerhart understood what Reimann wanted. The two of them moved away from the rest of the party but kept the city, and the advancing horde within sight.

When they were out of earshot of the battle-weary soldiers Gerhart said, 'What is it?'

'I believe that you have some understanding of the ways of battle,' the captain said, almost begrudgingly.

'Indeed I do,' Gerhart declared. 'I thought you would have seen that for yourself by now.'

'Then I would like to hear what you suggest we do now,' Reimann said, running a hand through his close-cropped grey hair. 'I know what I would do, but I would like to see if we concur.'

'Is it not obvious? We pursue this to the end,' Gerhart declared boldly. 'We take the fight to the enemy, harry them from behind and do all we can to stop them succeeding in their task, or die trying.'

'My men are weary. They have been pushed to the limits of their endurance.'

Gerhart could see that Karl Reimann was a good man and a worthy captain. He had the well-being of his men at heart but never showed any signs of weakness in front of them.

'With but a push in the right direction, even the slowest soldiers can find the way to greatness,' the wizard said gruffly.

'To a soldier, the only thing more treacherous than the battle itself is the expanse of open ground yet to be won,' Reimann countered.

The captain was obviously tired himself after their recent exertions. Gerhart felt it too, and more keenly with the worsening of the weather, but they could not let it beat them. Not now.

The bright wizard looked back to the city. The flickering beams and bars of the Northland lights had intensified, exuding a malign phosphorescence not unlike the light cast by the sickly Chaos moon Morrslieb. The eerie luminescence lit the night for miles around.

A distant rumble rolled across the hills and the blanket of the forest, but it was unlike the growl of thunder. It was as if the storm had a voice, a booming voice that spoke of the coming of the End Times, the doom of nations and annihilation of all mortal races. And it was getting colder, much colder.

The storm of Chaos was upon them.

VENDHAL SCREAMED THE words of the incantation in dark tongue. They cut through the gale and the roar of the wind with their cruel timbre.

The Chaos sorcerer was only half-aware of his pronouncements. It was as if he was so saturated with power now that he had transcended his mortal body and was looking down on the scene as he neared the climax of the ritual.

The runes on the ground flickered and writhed. He stood at the heart of it all, the glittering skull raised high above his head, the winds of magic swirling around him in a tumbling tumult. He had thrust his staff into the ground next to him. The stones set into the sockets of the iron skull surmounting it were glowing a malevolent red, like his own eyes. The orb-wand tucked into his belt pulsed with a throbbing, cold blue light. Power soared into him.

Overhead the storm clouds sparked with barely-contained lightning. They roiled and writhed like things given unnatural life by the warping magical energies saturating the environment. The very air seemed to thicken around him.

For a moment he felt as if the power of the building storm was more than he could bear, as if he was about to unleash a force upon the world that was so devastating it could not be controlled by a mere mortal.

But Vendhal Skullwarper was no mere Northern shaman. He felt that he was no longer even just a sorcerer of Chaos. He was something much greater. He was the chosen channel of the power of the Dark Gods of Chaos, who dwelt beyond space, time and the comprehension of primitive mortal minds.

Vendhal threw back his head and looked up into the vortex of power surging above him. He luxuriated in the energising essence of the magical forces gathering there.

'The power of Chaos is mine!' the sorcerer screamed to the tortured heavens.

With a howl like a hundred packs of hungry wolves, the winter storm rushed in and the warping power of Chaos tore through the summer night. The wail of the tempest drowned the excited cheers of the Kurgan as the power of the north laid siege to Wolfenburg.

Snow did not so much fall as sweep across the countryside in a whirling wall of white. In no time at all thick frost covered the landscape for a league in every direction and ice, growing upon thrashing branches in minutes, weighed down the trees of the surrounding spurs of woodland.

Then the night exploded.

Forked lightning clawed the sky, striking the city walls like repeated hammer blows rained down by a storm giant. Masonry exploded from the stonework where the lightning lashed at the curtain wall with flashing talons of actinic white energy.

This was the power of the Dark Gods in all its terrifying glory. Nothing could stand before the might and the supremacy of raw Chaos.

With a roar like the crashing scream of a landslide the ancient gatehouse of the city, which had withstood attacks for two thousand years, collapsed in an avalanche of rock and stone. Men fell screaming to their deaths, crushed by the very battlements that they were sworn to defend.

The city had been breached.

Jeering and yelling, the Northmen needed no command to drive them on. Bellowing their battle cries the marauders galloped and ran towards the fractured city walls. In a great black tide, Surtha Lenk's barbarian horde broke open Wolfenburg and began to put everyone inside to the sword. They exacted their bloodthirsty revenge on those who had denied them their prize and the glory of battle for so long.

With coruscating tendrils of magic whipping about him still, Vendhal Skullwarper stepped from his circle of runes and joined the advance. Wherever he trod, the ground wept tears of blood, in response to the Chaos power that infused every fibre of his being.

Following the rampaging Chaos horde, the sorcerer strode into the blighted city. Icicles hung from the eaves of buildings, their roofs laden with heavy falls of snow. Ice crunched underfoot, melting with a sizzling hiss wherever he walked.

The wintry winds were now beginning to give way to something far more Chaotic altogether. Such was the warping way of the great mutator; nothing remained free from the effects of change for long. Almost as abruptly as it had begun, the blizzard ceased but the storm did not abate. Tendrils of Chaotic power began to snake down from the seething clouds, striking like lightning. Only unlike the caress of lightning, these strange tendrils had an altogether different effect.

Vendhal watched with unalloyed pleasure as a coil of cloud, rippling with all the colours of the visible spectrum, whipped down from the boiling sky. The warping tendril struck the side of a house. Where it hit, the wall was stone no longer. Instead, something more akin to dark purple flesh bubbled and blistered there.

Another tendril struck, earthing itself against the cobbles of the street. As the power discharged, bulbous, glistening eyes blinked in terror from the stones and gaping, leech mouths opened and closed in the road spasmodically.

A woman ran screaming from the crumbling ruins of a lightning blasted house. Vendhal watched as her foot snagged in an opening leech-mouth and she fell onto her hands and knees. Another twisting tendril of energy lashed down from the storm and struck the woman. Her cries became a harsh, braying wail as her whole body underwent a terrifying transformation.

The woman's legs became boneless, rubbery tentacles. One arm sloughed its skin and became a serpentine protuberance, her hand now a fanged maw. Her other arm sprouted iridescent feathers and became a flapping wing. Great clumps of hair fell from her scalp as her head swelled and contracted again. It was as if something was writhing inside her skull trying to claw its way out.

Vendhal walked past the woman with a sick smile on his lips. He was revelling in the glorious changes wrought by Tzeentch upon Wolfenburg. The thing that was left after this terrible transformation fortunately did not survive much longer.

The sorcerer knew well the stories of what had happened to the city of Praag in Kislev after the attack of Asavar Kul. Once he was finished with Wolfenburg, Praag would seem like a mere experiment. The sentinel city would become the new renowned masterpiece of Chaos.

Across the street, houses burned amidst the last flurries of snow. Vendhal raised his skull-staff and pointed at a man fleeing from the Chaos looters. He still clutched the pearlescent skull in his other hand. Another bolt of warping energy seared down from the fiery clouds, blasting the sorcerer's victim from his feet. The man tumbled to a halt against the side of a building, from which blinked tearful eyes. The man now resembled something more like a toad, with a forked whip-tongue, cockerel's wattles and scuttling crab legs.

Truly he, Vendhal Skullwarper, was the chosen of Tzeentch. He was luxuriating in the raw stuff of Chaos that wreathed his body, heightened his senses, and raised his mind to unparalleled levels of consciousness.

Surtha Lenk was nothing compared to him. The high zar was not even fit to lick the filth from the soles of his boots.

When the doom of the Dark Gods had been wrought upon the city of Wolfenburg, Vendhal Skullwarper would show the Kurgan horde who commanded the warping storms of Chaos. They would see who the true messiah of the great sorcerer was.

THE BLIZZARD HAD abated as swiftly as it had arisen. In its wake, the rag-tag survivors of Karl's regiment, along with the glowering wizard, had made it as far as the city and were now following the Chaos horde, trying to find a way into Wolfenburg.

Ahead of Karl's party, the last of the barbarians were making their way into the city through a shattered gap in the lightning-blasted curtain wall. It was plain to the life-long soldier that these were the runts of the marauder horde; those who had followed the tribes as they moved south in the hope of sharing in the glory of conquest but having little to offer themselves. They were the weakest, feeblest and oldest among the camp followers.

The Northland lights still flickered over the burning rooftops of Wolfenburg, bathing the snow-covered landscape for miles around with their spectral luminescence. It seemed to Karl that the weather itself had been possessed by some Chaos power, as tornado-like spirals of cloud swooped down from the broiling multi-hued mass of the thunderheads.

A sound like thunder rumbled across the city, but to the veteran Reiklander it sounded more like the snarling of some feral beast. Unnerved by what was happening, Karl looked to the ruddy-robed wizard.

There was fire in the mage's eyes. The bright wizard paused at the fissure in the curtain wall as the acrid stench of burning washed over the party. The mage inhaled deeply, closing his eyes, almost as if in ecstasy. Gerhart held his oak staff tightly in his left hand. In his right he held a sword that one of the Imperial soldiers had given him. It had belonged to one of their fellows who had fallen battling the daemon engine's protectors. The wizard's straggly grey-black hair flicked and writhed in the unnatural winds that blew through the gap in the city wall. He looked every part the avenging hero of old. Perhaps there was hope for them all yet.

Then the screaming began.

At first the city's terrified townsfolk thought that the daemonic howls were an effect of the unnatural storm battering Wolfenburg. But the sinister, unearthly cries continued and panicking eyes were turned towards the heavens.

Lashes of fluctuating indigo, blue and yellow energy were coiling down from the storm clouds, making the tempest look like some sky-borne ancient kraken of legend. Other things were also escaping from the roiling clouds: creatures born of nightmares, all teeth and talons, carried on bat-wings like ragged shrouds.

The creatures descended in a squabbling flock, falling on the fleeing townspeople. These were the furies. Their flickering shadows swept over the snow-covered, burning streets.

The distraught defenders did their best to fend off the furies' attacks but they were terribly outnumbered. Men were lifted off the ground, yelling, in the taloned grips of the flying beasts. They were carried, struggling, high above the rooftops only to be dropped again.

Before they even hit the ground, many of the poor wretches were caught by other diving furies and torn apart in mid-air by the savage, hellish creatures.

Those who did manage to escape the clutching talons of the leathery-winged daemons found other, equally horrific things emerging from the smoke and fires. Where the warping-lightning struck, great fire-spouting wyrms had grown, their bodies lengthening as they absorbed the magical energies saturating the air of the city. Gangly-limbed things capered and danced in a seething sea of eldritch energy, their pink and blue-skinned forms never constant as mystical energy seethed through them. They were Chaos unbound given physical form.

What many saw within this scion of hell drove them into madness.

A tall figure moved awkwardly through the running rabble. He was swathed in a thick black cloak, his face hidden by the heavy cowl. As he watched the chaos unfurling all around him he gibbered and giggled to himself, seemingly unconcerned by this vision of hell. Instead, every so often he patted something secured under his tightly drawn cloak.

The stranger had been mad long before the Realm of Chaos descended on Wolfenburg and made the city a domain of daemons.

THE HALBERDIERS, THEIR commander and the fire mage, forced their way further into the madness that was Wolfenburg, cutting down blood-crazed marauders and wild-eyed maniacs every step of the way.

The stricken city was like a living, vibrant vision of one of the paintings of the heretical artist Beronymous Hosch. Buildings burned, men and women, old and young, were put to the slaughter, and screams rent the greasy air.

All around them the Northmen put people to the sword, whilst daemonic entities that had no right to exist in the mortal realm feasted on the bodies and souls of innocent and sinner alike. It was all the soldiers could do to keep from losing their minds as well. But their captain was a veteran of countless battles, many against the unnatural thrall-servants of the Chaos powers. As long as he stood firm in the face of the enemy, then so would his men.

The seething crowds of marauding barbarians, embattled defenders and fleeing townspeople parted and Gerhart and the others suddenly found themselves in an area of relative calm. They were in a square. It was as if they had reached the eye of the storm, of this storm of Chaos.

They were not alone. On the other side of the square stood a figure, silhouetted against the backdrop of burning buildings. The figure was draped in a long, hooded cloak, almost the same colour as the robes worn by the fire mage. Gerhart could see at once that this was no pyromancer of the Bright order. The man also wore brass armour adorned with leering, gargoyle faces, and runes that glowed with an eerie inner light. They left no doubt as to where the man's loyalties lay.

Gerhart could see immediately that the stranger was alive with the raw power of Chaos-magic. It came off him in pulsing waves; enough to make the world around him shimmer in a heat haze. Gerhart could see it in the glowing red gem-eyes of the sorcerer's iron-skull staff, in the man's own burning stare, and in the glowing sockets of the polished human skull gripped in his other clawed hand. The closer Gerhart looked, the more it seemed that the eyes of the pearlescent skull flickered in time with the storm writhing in the sky.

And there was something else. To Gerhart's mage-sight it seemed that the Chaos sorcerer was draining the magical essences of the winds of magic.

Gerhart was convinced that it was this sorcerer who was responsible for the Chaotic storm. Ribbons of swirling magical energy linked the man to the turmoil above, and the enchanted skull was the key to the spell.

Gerhart knew what had to be done.

In his mind's eye, and in the presence of the hungry flames and the growing power of Aqshy that was drawn to the burning city, the candle-flame was no more. Instead it was a fiercely blazing brand. Gerhart could feel warmth being transmitted through his body as well as the heat of the fires all around him, suffusing him with their power, their majesty and their might.

Seeing what had become of the ancient sentinel city, frustrated that the council of war had not followed his advice, and angered that he had been sent away from Wolfenburg when the city needed him most, Gerhart had fuelled the fire of his fury and hatred. This in turn fed the fires burning within him, and the flame of Aqshy.

The fury the pyromancer would unleash upon the Chaos sorcerer would be like nothing the self-satisfied villain had ever known, nor would ever know again.

Meanwhile, the fell sorcerer held the glimmering skull above his head and began to utter some vile incantation in the cursed language of those blasphemous entities that existed beyond the boundaries of the mortal realm.

The two spell-casters faced one another across the square. The Chaos sorcerer seemed unconcerned by the ten halberdiers. He was wholly focused on the bright wizard who stood braced, staff outstretched, sword in hand, ready to duel.

But then Reimann's men had their own battles to fight. As if drawn to the heart of Chaos, warp-changed Chaos spawn crawled and slithered through the corridors of flame that were the burning streets of Wolfenburg.

The Chaos sorcerer laughed mirthlessly as he witnessed their predicament.

HEARING A SCRAPING behind him, like plate mail dragged over cobbles, Karl turned. Dragging itself towards him across the square was something that had obviously once been a man. From the chest up it was still human, whimpering and moaning in agony and horror. From the waist down, the poor wretch had been changed utterly. His lower body had developed a hardened carapace that looked like armoured plates. His legs had become swollen, veiny-fleshed arms, his feet now clawed, three-fingered hands. No matter what his broken mind might will, the lower half of his body was reacting to some other sentience as it heaved its bulk forwards.

And there were other things too creeping, scuttling and sliding towards them. Things with feathers, claws and fungoid bodies. Things with too many bony limbs and too many gaping mouths. There was something that looked like two people merged, but they were joined in such a way that it was no longer possible to tell which limbs had belonged to which half. The skin covering the Chaos twins looked like melted wax and was striped with great red weals as if it had been under the lash.

The Reiklanders moved away from the wizard's side to more defensible positions. The fire mage was on his own now and Karl prayed that the wizard was a match for the corrupted sorcerer.

An arachnoid abomination, bloated and covered in matted fur, but displaying a fanged human face with ophidian eyes in the centre of its body, skittered down the side of an untouched building. It leapt several yards in one bound to get close to the infantrymen.

Karl realised that this might very well be the last battle he ever fought. He was determined to make it count and sell his life dear, as would all of his men. This was what they had been born to, the life of a soldier was the only life any of them had ever known. Karl couldn't imagine meeting his end any other way.

'Come on, boys!' the old Reiklander captain shouted grimly over the tumult of the warp storm. 'This is it. This could be our last stand. Make it count!'

Shouting the war cry of the armies of the Reik, the halberdiers prepared to sell their souls at a very high price indeed.

SPELLS ROARED FROM the hands and staffs of the two wizards like screaming skull-face comets. They streaked through the tortured air as the Chaos sorcerer and the Imperial wizard each tried to bring ruin upon each other. Arcane gestures and sweeps of their magical totems lessened their impact.

A raging inferno swirled around them, sparking eddies of power bursting from the mage-storm and exploding like firecrackers in the air. The flames leapt higher, as if in response to the fury of the magical duel being waged in the square. Every building around them was burning now, like a fiery barricade that kept other players in the battle at bay.

As they battled in their unreal otherworld of sorcery, the unnatural light of the spectral storm overhead combined with the blasts of their spells to illuminate the two combatants.

The Chaos sorcerer was so suffused with magical power that nothing Gerhart did seemed to touch him. They would fight on until exhaustion eventually claimed one of them. Gerhart feared he would be the first to tire. For while the sorcerer had the fearsome skull in his possession the winds of magic were drawn straight to him, to fuel his spells as well as his magical defences. Thanks to the barrage of sorcery directed at him by the warp-enchanter, Gerhart could not get near enough to his opponent to disrupt his spell-casting.

Gerhart was on the verge of losing his temper but he somehow managed to focus his mind and keep a tight rein on his powers. He feared – he knew – that if he lost control now, with the Chaos storm raging above him, he too could go too far into his own magic and never be able to return. He would become a feral thing like the creature he had encountered in the hills above Keulerdorf. And if that happened Chaos would have his soul and what semblance remained of his humanity. His individuality and personality would be swallowed up in a haze of soul-destroying madness. Gerhart Brennend would not allow that to become his fate.

The heroic effort he was making to remain in control was costing him dear. In spite of the wind of Aqshy surging through him, he still felt himself weakening with every spell he cast. Gerhart did not know how much longer he could keep his efforts up for.

He was only vaguely aware of the Reiklanders battling the Chaos spawn around them. He was becoming more and more aware of the bone-aching weariness that threatened to overwhelm him. Then, weakened, with his guard down, the Chaos sorcerer would step in for the kill, no doubt savouring the moment of victory.

The burning brand inside his mind began to sputter and spark fitfully. Gerhart sensed that he could only really channel one more spell before he was spent.

Then it came to him, as lucidity comes to an old man on his deathbed, when there is nothing more that can be said or done.

Gerhart staggered backwards, leaning on his staff for support. The flame trailing from the end of the oaken bough coughed and went out. Perverse satisfaction flashed in the Chaos sorcerer's unblinking, coal-eyed stare. The bright wizard sagged to his knees on the hot cobbles of the square. His nemesis took a step towards him.

'Before I kill you it is only right that you should know the name of the one who has robbed you of your strength, your art and your life, so that when your soul has become the plaything of daemons you will be tormented for all eternity by the knowledge,' the Chaos sorcerer declared cruelly. 'I am Vendhal Skull-warper and the warping storms of Chaos are mine to command!' the sorcerer pronounced, his voice rising above the howling of the storm and its Chaos-spawned offspring.

'And I,' growled a sweat-streaming Gerhart, 'am Gerhart Brennend, pyromancer of the Bright order and keeper of the keys of Azimuth. Now burn in hell, you bastard!' and with that the fire mage released the spell he had been holding back – one last magical missile that burned with the intense heat of a volcano.

The monstrous fireball, a flame-wreathed screaming skull of a comet, blasted at the sorcerer, hitting him with all the force of a meteorite crashing to earth. Possessed of a supreme arrogance in his own abilities, the gloating sorcerer had fallen for Gerhart's piece of ham acting, and had left himself open to a close range attack.

Vendhal Skullwarper was sent flying through the whirling air by the impact of the fireball and smashed through the burning bricks and mortar of a building. With a ravenous roar, the blazing timbers of the structure's roof gave way, crashing down on the sorcerer in a great cloud of blossoming sparks.

For a moment Gerhart believed he had stopped the master of the Chaos storm, but the wreckage of the burning building was thrown clear and the Chaos sorcerer strode out of the ruins, his body seemingly unharmed. He was surrounded by an aura of writhing multi-coloured energy, the ever-changing colours looking like the swirling spectrum of oil on water.

So charged with magic was Vendhal Skullwarper that Gerhart's final, most powerful spell had not caused him any damage at all.

But it had made him drop the glittering skull.

KARL WITNESSED THE blow the Imperial wizard dealt the sorcerer, and saw the servant of Chaos hurtle through the wall of the burning building, the malignant skull flying from his grasp. Then, in horror, he watched the sorcerer rise from the ashes, apparently unharmed.

The gleaming skull landed with a clatter amongst the scalding cobbles and scattered pieces of burning material. He did not fully understand why, but Karl knew that he had to get hold of the skull before the Chaos sorcerer did.

With a sharp thrust of his gore-encrusted halberd, the veteran soldier dispatched the half-fish thing that was hopping towards him, hissing like a serpent, opening its belly with a deft twist of his weapon. Something akin to stinking broth gushed from the wound. There did not appear to be any solid organs amongst the mess. Karl forced his tired leg muscles into a sprint, desperation and adrenaline lending him strength.

Karl reached the spot where the skull lay just in time to kick it from the grasp of a slime-exuding, tentacled thing. With a sharp thrust he brought the heavy haft of his weapon down on top of the shimmering-hued bony object.

There was a crack like a thunderclap as the skull exploded and Karl was lifted off his feet to crash to the ground again several yards away as the warp storm went berserk.

WITH THE DESTRUCTION of the Chaos sorcerer's potent talisman, it was not only the warping storm that changed as the link holding it all together was broken.

The sorcerer was screaming, his shrill, high-pitched shrieks cutting through the voice of the storm like a bell. His cloak streamed out behind him, and he became the focus of the storm's rage.

Something else was happening to the sorcerer as well.

Gerhart saw it most clearly in the man's puffy grey features. The flesh there rippled like the wind-blown surface of a lake. The fire faded from the sorcerer's eyes, which now bulged and retracted as the warping power flooded through every part of his body searching for a means of escape.

Unable to contain the raw warping energy surging through it, Vendhal Skullwarper's body reached breaking point and warped out. Arms and legs twisted at unnatural angles. Other bones and joints bent out of shape, thrusting at the man's deforming flesh from inside. His staff was torn from his grasp and spun away.

Still screaming, the mutating Chaos sorcerer was carried up into the spiralling vortex by hurricane force winds. He was sucked up into the heart of the storm, his body twisting horribly out of shape in excruciating throes, until he was no more than a dark speck against the flickering, roiling, unnatural clouds.

Gerhart gradually became conscious of a shout coming from the soldiers still battling around them. It was the Reikland captain. 'We have to get out of here, now!' the veteran soldier was screaming.

The bright wizard glanced up at the boiling clouds above him. The thunderheads had darkened to purple like a spreading bruise, and the clouds roiled like milk poured into water. The Chaos sorcerer was gone, Wolfenburg had been razed and there was nothing more that they could do now.

With the command, the survivors of the halberdier regiment, several sporting gaping wounds delivered by scything claws, brutal fangs and contusions caused by constricting tentacles or pseudopods, rallied. Reimann prepared to lead his men out of the city again. The howling hurricane had blown out many of the flames so that now a way could be navigated between the burning buildings. Gerhart, exhaustion threatening to overwhelm him, leaning heavily on his staff for support, turned to follow.

A new sound came to his ears over the whining of the wind and the crackling of the flames. Hearing an insane giggling, the wizard turned. Behind him, on the other side of the square, standing between two burning buildings, was a figure wearing an all-enveloping cloak.

'Gerhart Brennend!' the stranger called. There was something familiar about the voice. 'We meet again.'

An arm emerged from the folds of the heavy cloak and the figure aimed the flintlock pistol at the fire wizard. With a ratcheting click the firearm was primed. The pyromancer had seen that weapon before. He had been in a similar position once before.

The cloaked stranger threw back the hood of his cloak to reveal the horribly disfigured, burn-scarred face beneath. Regardless of the terrible changes that had been wrought upon the man's body, there was enough about him for Gerhart to recognise the man as being his one-time judge, jury and would-be executioner, the witch hunter Gottfried Verdammen.

Verdammen's manner retained nothing of its previous composure. It was apparent to Gerhart that the terrible burns the witch hunter had suffered at the fire wizard's hands, and all that he had witnessed since from within Wolfenburg had driven him insane. How had he even survived his fireball spell, Gerhart found himself wondering?

Verdammen giggled again, a disconcerting, childish sound. 'I won't miss this time,' he said, and fired the pistol.

There was no way of avoiding the shot and the bullet found its mark. Gerhart was spun round by the force of the impact and went down, falling into the ruins of a burning house.

The witch hunter's hysterical laughter ceased abruptly as the fire mage rose from the flames like the legendary phoenix of Arabian myth, born again from the fires of its own destruction.

Gerhart's robes had caught fire. His eyes blazed and balls of scintillating flame surrounded his bunched fists. The flames of the burning building flickered and writhed, forming a roaring vortex of fire with the pyromancer at its heart. Dark blood dribbled from the bullet-hole in the wizard's shoulder.

At first the terribly scarred witch hunter's face fell, then the hysterical laughter returned. Verdammen was still cackling like an inmate of an asylum when the smouldering fire mage cast his spell.

Racing, writhing flames burst from the wizard's stabbing fingertips, eating up the space between the mage and the witch hunter. By the time the conjuration reached Verdammen it had become a roiling ball of fire that burst around him in a molten flood. Clothes, hair and skin charred, sizzled and blistered as Gerhart obliterated his nemesis in a fiery, bone-burning conflagration.

Within seconds the searing blast turned the witch hunter into a blackened skeleton and a cloud of whirling ash that was carried up to the heavens by the ascending thermals. As the furious blast furnace roar of the flames died so at last it seemed did the madman's hysterical laughter.

And with that, the temper that Gerhart had struggled so hard to control burst like a ruptured dam. The searing pain of the bullet wound he had sustained had been the final straw. The one thing that he had tried so hard to prevent had come to pass. He lost control of the raging magic coursing through his veins like molten magma.

Fires raged.

Wolfenburg burned.

And all hell was let loose once again as the pain-maddened pyromancer went on the rampage like a man possessed.

TWELVE
Winds of Change

*'And I saw before me a barren plain under a burn-
ing sky that was bathed in swirling, surging
energies. I knew that this was the source of all
energy employed by practitioners of the sorcerous
arts, the place that is so crudely known as the
Realm of Chaos. There was a disturbance in the
forces and a tendril of energy lashed from the
seething currents, breaking free and flowing out
over the twisted plain.*

*'I felt I was racing over the world, following the
writhing tendril, but now it seemed to my mind's
eye more like a wind, only a wind made of impossible colours, that chose their own course as they
blew over ice-capped mountains, stormy seas and
brooding forests.*

*And at last I found myself descending with the
magical winds to those places where the dead lie,*

*and my heart was heavy for then I understood the
truth of the fate that awaits all those who would
practise the art of magic.'*

– From the *Liber Hereticus*, Chapter LVIII,
'Galdrath's Vision'

AUTUMN HAD COME at last and the prevailing wind
stopped blowing from the north and began to blow
the last warmth of summer from the south. The leaves
on the trees curled from emerald to gold.

Several days had passed since the sacking of Wolfenburg by Surtha Lenk's Chaos horde. The Northmen
had run through the city streets putting everyone they
found to the sword to the glory of their dark masters
and setting all the buildings to the torch in their wake.
Much of the ancient, sentinel city had been razed to
the ground thanks to the machinations of the marauders, the intervention of terrifyingly powerful sinister
entities, and the subsequent fire that had spread
rapidly through the close-packed streets and half-tim-
bered buildings.

The morning after, the warbands had raised their
hateful skull-stacks outside the broken curtain wall on
the mud-churned meadow at the bend in the river.
They baptised them with the blood of further human
sacrifices, souls slaughtered in a second massacre,
almost as horrendous as that which had occurred the
night before. They spent the rest of the day celebrating
the downfall of their landmark conquest, singing blasphemous hymns of praise to their vile patron gods,
and lauding the fell powers.

Those who had survived the breaking of the city had
fled north-west away from the rampaging Chaos

horde. These same refugees – soldiers mainly, their units broken and routed – knew there was nothing they could do now to drive back the invaders other than regroup and plan their next course of action. Some townsfolk joined them in their flight, only stopping when the city and the shouts and screams of the Kurgan war company were a memory, echoing in their ears. Once they reached the foothills of the great mist-shrouded foothills of the Middle Mountains and they made camp there.

The surviving soldiers, under the command of the veteran Reiklander Karl Reimann, had taken turns to keep watch, manning a border guard around the temporary camp within the ruins of a ruined sheep farm. They took turns to keep watch from their strong vantage point on the slope of a hill and looked down over the canopy of the brooding forest to the smoking devastation that had once been the mightiest of the northern marcher strongholds.

The toppled towers and fire-gutted brick shells that had once been buildings could quite clearly be seen, even from almost a league away. Drifts of white-grey smoke, the colour of dead flesh, washed over the brittle ruins and through the gaps in the lightning-blackened curtain wall. The castle of the elector count of Ostland was now nothing more that a skeletal shell. Fires still burned within the castle. None among the survivors hailed from among Valmir von Raukov's household, and none knew of the Elector Count's fate.

The writhing Chaos-possessed storm had finally consumed itself, blowing itself out when the Chaos sorcerer who had summoned it disappeared. With the first light of dawn the following day, winter had been banished again. The snow and ice thawed to slush with the changing of the seasons and the ambient heat of the burning city. By late afternoon there was hardly a drift of cloud left in the Nachgeheim sky.

Now, days later, much of the fire that had ravaged the city had burnt itself out too. There had been nothing anyone could do, with the Chaos horde in command of the land around Wolfenburg, other than leave the fire to take its course. Some buildings still smouldered and smoked even now. The ancient sentinel city had been razed to the ground.

Gerhart Brennend sniffed the air. The soft, decaying touch of autumn showed in the surrounding landscape, particularly in the turning leaves of the blankets of woodland. The air was turning colder, and it bore the smoky odour of bonfires. The land was in the grip of leaf-fall.

He too had burnt himself out, collapsing at last amidst the fire-blasted ruins of a guild house, his powers spent and his body physically exhausted. At least that which he feared so greatly – of going so far into the grip of his sorcery that there was no way back – had not come to pass. However, when he woke and his senses returned, so did the overwhelming feelings of shame and guilt that he had lost control of his temper.

He had left Wolfenburg in the wake of many of those now huddled within the refugee camp, and had been one of the last to reach the Imperial encampment. He had trudged up to the cordon of sentry-guards from among Captain Reimann's halberdiers, who took a while to recognise him, as his face, hair and robes were stained black with soot. He resembled a ravening flagellant of the Cult of Sigmar more than a grand battle-wizard of the colleges of magic. No one else had joined the refuge for the last two days. There would be no others now.

Captain Reimann approached Gerhart. The fire wizard would not claim for one minute that the halberdier captain had been pleased to see him, but Reimann at least acknowledged his presence after all they had experienced. Gerhart still felt, however, that the Reiklander didn't really trust him.

Even now, inside the camp, Gerhart sat apart from the other refugees who were sitting in a huddled, shocked silence.

As Gerhart looked down on the distant smoking ruins he was reminded, with a gut-twisting pang of guilt, of Wollestadt. It had been his family's home for generations. Gerhart's elder brother had been groomed to take over the family's wool business from their Averland father. Gerhart, the second son, had been sent to Altdorf to study at the colleges of magic when he displayed some aptitude for scholarship and magic. In time his father retired and Gerhart's brother had taken over the business. Gerhart gradually lost contact with his family, as he rose through the ranks of the Bright order, from apprentice to respected battle-wizard.

However, when Wollestadt had come under threat from the skaven vermin-kin, Gerhart had been at the head of the Imperial army that was sent to deal with the vile ratmen. When the Imperial troops arrived and saw how the town had already been desecrated by the skaven, Gerhart had lost his temper. In his haste and wrath he brought the fiery wrath of Aqshy to bear against the children of the horned rat. The winds of magic blew strongly over the Averland downs that day and fanned the fire left in the wake of

Gerhart's magical attacks so that the close-packed buildings of the town had caught alight.

The skaven were denied their victory but the conflagration grew, consuming the whole town. The disaster came to be known as the Great Fire of Wollestadt. The Imperial rescuers, and the town's populace who could escape, retreated. The cost had been high indeed but Gerhart believed the ends had justified the means. The greater good had been served and the skaven destroyed.

It was only later that Gerhart discovered his whole family had burnt to death amidst the flames, including his father, brother and his brother's family. The Brennend line had been completely wiped out. He had destroyed the very people he should have saved.

People had been shocked and appalled by what the fire wizard had done. From that time on he had lived with the guilt of the knowledge that he had caused the deaths of his family as well as much of the populace of Wollestadt, not to mention the destruction of the town itself.

He had been vilified for what he had done and exiled from ranks of the battle-mages of the Empire. He had left the Bright college taking up the life of a wandering wizard, trying to make amends for what he had done, by fighting the Empire's enemies where he found them. At first he had seriously considered relinquishing his kommission and never using his magic again but he had been unable to abstain – it was bound to every fibre of his being, and had been for many years. But Gerhart had always feared that one day he might lose control of his powers again, with reason, as it had turned out.

* * *

TALK AND RUMOUR were rife within the camp as the survivors tried to make sense of all that had happened. They were starting to gather updated information regarding the deployment of the enemy. They were also desperate for news of other Imperial forces that might come to their aid still, even after so long. They could not believe that news of what had befallen Wolfenburg would not have reached the ears of other Imperial commanders and that they wouldn't send their own troops to their aid.

Some said that the other great cities of the Empire had also been beset by the invading Chaos armies. There was also talk of the Kislevites mobilising to fulfil old vows that they had once sworn to Ostland. Some said that the Grand Theogonist Volkmar had been slaughtered as he led a crusade into the bleak lands of the Troll Country. It was even rumoured that the Emperor Karl-Franz himself was dead, killed in battle.

So it was that the survivors sent out their own scouts to find out what was happening.

And that morning, two scouts – wearing the livery of the elector count's standing army, and wearing the badges of their injuries, like medals, with pride – had returned to the camp and reported what they had found. Huddles of people, civilian and soldier alike, gathered around at their arrival, as they made their report to Captain Reimann.

'They're turning back,' the burlier of the two said as he dismounted from the horse he had been riding, his face a mess of swellings and livid bruises.

'They're leaving?' Karl asked.

'Yes,' the second scout confirmed. He was leaner and shorter than his partner. 'They've abandoned the charnel house they've made of Wolfenburg and are definitely heading back north towards Kislev. Every warband, and they are taking their infernal siege engines with them, their camp followers, their beasts, everything.'

'They are all leaving?' Karl repeated.

'All. All are heading north.'

'There was just one group we saw heading south from the fringes of the Forest of Shadows towards Wolfenburg,' the second scout pointed out.

'What? Who are they?'

'We couldn't tell, captain.'

'Were they on horseback?' Karl asked.

'One of them is, sir.'

'Are they adjuncts to the main Chaos horde?'

'Unlikely. I thought they looked more like holy men.'

'Could they be Chaos cultists?'

'It is possible,' the burly scout agreed.

'But whatever they are, they're heading this way.'

'And whoever they are, they carry the Wolfenburg Standard.'

THE CURTAIN WALL of the once great city rose up before the warrior priest's party like the blackened and broken teeth of a giant. Beyond the fractured fortifications smoke continued to rise. Lector Wilhelm Faustus stopped. His entourage, numbering only six, came to a halt behind him.

The priest said nothing as he surveyed the ruins of the city through his one good eye. His features were set grim like the carved image of one of the statues of the Heldenhammer in the grand temple of Sigmar in Alt-dorf. The Wolfenburg Standard flapped vainly in the autumnal breeze.

The lector had been right. The doom he had predicted had indeed visited Wolfenburg. In spite of all they had achieved in recovering the legendary war banner from the unruly beastherd, they were too late to save the city.

The legends had been right after all; the fabled Wolfenburg Standard had been lost and Wolfenburg had fallen.

For the first time in a long time, despair welled up in the weary priest's heart. A less devout and god-fearing man might have begun to doubt the power of the Lord Sigmar. It truly seemed that the End Times were here. But this wasn't over, not by a long way.

'Your holiness,' one of the zealots said, daring to break the silence. 'The city has fallen. What should we do now?'

'This is what the infamous city of the damned must have looked like,' Wilhelm said distantly, as if he had not heard the man's question.

'I beg your pardon, your grace?'

'After Sigmar's Hammer – the comet – struck Mordheim.'

'Lector!' another of the priest's followers called out, breaking through his reverie. 'Riders!'

He was aware of a drumming sound. Galloping down the slope of the hill to the west of the city was a party of riders matching the warrior priest's entourage man for man. From this distance he could not yet discern features and uniform, but from what Wilhelm had seen of the Chaos horde's foul behaviour he thought it unlikely that they would be sympathetic to the priest's cause.

Wilhelm prepared to make one last stand. He doubted that his exhausted and battle-weary warriors could prevail now. They had had to fight too hard and for too long already.

The riders were rapidly closing the distance between them, bearing down on the dishevelled troop of the holy man and his henchmen. Wilhelm hefted his warhammer into position and kicked Kreuz into a gallop. He was holding the Wolfenburg Standard aloft in his other hand. He thanked Sigmar that his steed had escaped the beastmen's predations and that the priest had been reunited with the noble Kreuz in his flight from the clearing.

'For Sigmar!' Wilhelm bellowed, his battle cry rolling out across the ruined meadow towards the approaching strangers. 'And for Wolfenburg!'

He would satisfy his anger at the atrocity that had been done to Sigmar's people and make these riders pay in blood and pain for their sins against god and man. Divine rage was on him now. He would not be stopped until all of the riders were dead or his own dead body had been trampled into the mud of the field by the savage, daemonic steeds.

Kreuz's hooves were pounding the ground too, and kicking up great clods of earth, closing the ground between the incensed priest and the unknown riders even more quickly. Wilhelm heard a faint cry, that was quickly whipped away from him by the wind in his ears. Then it came again.

'Lector Faustus,' the voice shouted. 'Those men are Imperial soldiers!'

'I HAD BEGUN to believe that with the fall of Wolfenburg all was lost, that the invaders would sweep through Ostland, burning all before them,' an elderly scholar was saying, 'until they were beating on the doors of the Emperor's palace in Altdorf.'

'Some say that the Chaos-lovers' dark messiah has set his sights on Middenheim,' a crossbowman reported miserably.

'Archaon?' the scholar scoffed. Those assembled around the campfire gasped and made the sign of the holy hammer or touched iron to ward against evil. 'The dread lord of the End Times is nothing but a bogeyman, a child's nursery phantom. There is no such one war-leader guiding the Chaos invasion. It is merely a group of like-minded opportunist warlords, their synchronous attacks working for each other's mutual benefit. They will fall upon each other before the year is out and the Empire will then be safe from their predations for another hundred years.'

'How can you stand there and say that,' the warrior priest growled, taking a step forward and putting an ironclad hand on the haft of his slung warhammer, 'after all you have seen?'

The scholar took a nervous step back and gulped audibly. 'I was merely saying that there could not possibly be one mortal man behind –'

'The mastermind behind this invasion is no mere man,' the priest interrupted. 'Of that I am certain. If you had witnessed what I have you would know to think otherwise.'

The scholar opened his mouth as if to speak again and then retreated back into the huddle around the campfire. He shied from the fierce glare on the face of the lector-priest and the survivors of his warband.

The atmosphere in the camp was one of shock, disbelief and denial. The people gathered there, Gerhart thought, had lived through the destruction of Wolfenburg and still couldn't quite come to terms with the fact that they were alive, or where they were supposed to go from this point. They had glimpsed hell and lived to tell the tale.

The scouts had returned to the encampment at the ravaged farm with the Sigmarites in tow. The arrival of the priest and his band had provoked mixed reactions. For many of the camp residents it brought a slim glimmer of hope, that there were still others out there, allied to their cause who sought to rid the land of Chaos. If there were these holy warriors, then there could be others too.

To the Sigmarites however, it seemed that their arrival at the refugee camp made the mood more grim. For their very existence reminded the warrior priest of the destruction of one of the ancient bastions of the Empire and how much had already been lost in this new war against Chaos. But at least they were all gathered together now and strategy could be discussed and subsequently acted upon.

'Permission to speak freely?' asked one of the Reiklanders from Captain Reimann's own band.

'Permission granted,' Reimann said.

'If the Northmen are returning to the unholy lands that spawned them, then the banishing of the accursed Chaos sorcerer that you and the mage achieved must have broken the Chaos horde. Without the warp-wizard's sorcery they are nothing,' the halberdier said. His tired ringed eyes had sunk into shadowy hollows, but they were now flashing with excitement.

'That's right,' another person agreed. 'Why else would they be turning on their heels now, after such a victory? What is to stop them simply marching onward into the heart of the Empire and ripping it out?'

'And with the Wolfenburg Standard returned, there is still hope,' a greatsword said.

'Yes, Wolfenburg will rise from the ashes once more,' a zealot proclaimed.

'Then it's over,' a young man wearing the outfit of an apprentice blacksmith said, tears of relief cutting channels through the grime covering his face. 'We can begin to rebuild our lives.'

'No, it is not over,' the bright wizard said, cutting in at last, countering the young smith's words. 'No, it is only just beginning. I can still sense the unease present in the winds of magic. Mark my words.'

Almost as one man, the people gathered around the campfire turned to look at the wizard on the edge of the circle. No one said anything but their looks said it all: despair, anger, grief, hatred. He had stolen the last glimmer of hope from their hearts, and for that they hated him almost as much as they hated the Chaos hordes that had robbed them of their homes, their livelihoods and their loved ones. Somewhere a child began to cry.

Gerhart knew he wasn't welcome here any more. The people didn't trust him. Even Reimann seemed to be avoiding him. For he had seen first hand, with his own eyes, what could happen when the fire mage lost control of his temper: and the wizard's temper was terrible, a feral beast that seemed untameable.

It had been in no small part thanks to him that the Chaos sorcerer had been banished. These people had claimed that his actions had helped save the day. But now that the battle was over it was plain that no one wanted him there any longer. The only reason that no one had told him so was because they feared him and what he might do. That fact stuck in Gerhart's craw in a knot of indescribable guilty pain that nothing could assuage.

Muttering to himself under his breath, the dishevelled wizard rose from the log he was sitting on, helping himself up with his staff. He felt old and tired. His body hadn't ached like this since the beating he had suffered at the hands of the witch hunter's torturer. Gerhart turned and walked away from the assembly at the campfire, heading west.

Nobody called after him, to ask him where he was going or to ask him to stay. In no time he was descending the hill towards the sheltering trees of the smoky woodland that clothed the foothills of the Middle Mountains and the land beyond as far as the eye could see.

A gentle breeze was picking up. It ruffled the straggly tangle of his hair and beard and worried at the hem of his robes.

The winds of change were blowing; Gerhart thought, and he would go where they took him. Somewhere others would be in need of a wizard's counsel.

Who knew what the future might bring, where it might take him?

And wherever he went, Gerhart knew, ultimately people's reactions would be the same. Trouble would never be far behind.

It was the way it had to be now. It was the way it would be forever more.

ABOUT THE AUTHOR

Jonathan Green works as a full-time teacher in West London. By night he relates tales of Torben Badenov's Kislevite mercenaries and the adventures of the Underhive bounty hunter Nathan Creed for *Inferno!* magazine. He became one of the Emperor's scribes in 1994 and has since penned a number of articles for *White Dwarf* and an ever-growing number of short stories for the Black Library.
Magestorm is his third novel.

More Jonathan Green from the Black Library

THE DEAD AND THE DAMNED

A Warhammer novel

TORBEN SWUNG HIS sword at the inhuman noble. The stroke opened a great gash across the vampire's chest through his shirt. The man stumbled backwards at the blow and collapsed over a gravestone.

'One down,' the mercenary said to himself with a grin, and span to face the other creatures.

Torben suddenly found himself hurled to the ground with the hissing nobleman furiously tearing at his mail armour with its talons. Twisting to one side, the warrior used his bulk to throw the clawing vampire from him. Quickly getting to his feet, he watched open-mouthed as the wound he had dealt the man closed bloodlessly before his very eyes.

BADENOV'S MERCENARIES *are a group of hard-bitten fighting men. Drawn from the length and breadth of the Empire, they are held together by a lust for gold and a thirst for glory. Vampires, ghouls, rat-men and the Dark Knights of Chaos all abound in this land, but Badenov and his men will battle on until the last of them joins the dead or the damned!*

More Jonathan Green from the Black Library

CRUSADE FOR ARMAGEDDON

A Warhammer 40,000 novel

THE BRUTE HAMMERED home its advantage, kicking out with an iron-shod foot. Ansgar's consecrated suit of biomechanically linked armour was less cumbersome than his aggressor's and he was able to react swiftly, side-stepping the kick. The Space Marine brought the crackling power sword around in a deft arc, the blade singing as its sheathing energy field cut through the molecules of the air.

There was a bright flash as Ansgar's weapon connected with the ork's armoured arm, slicing cleanly through a bundle of power cables. The snapping callipers of the claw closed.

MARSHALL BRANT of the Black Templars returns home after leading his Space Marines through countless campaigns. But all hopes of respite soon fade when they find their planet, Solemnus, under savage attack. After a desperate struggle, Brant finds his forces are all but destroyed and the honour of the Chapter stained with blood. His vow for revenge takes him to the fiery shores of Armageddon, a sulphurous world synonymous with war, and into the heat of battle!

More Warhammer from the Black Library

THE GOTREK & FELIX NOVELS

by William King

THE DWARF TROLLSLAYER Gotrek Gurnisson and his long-suffering human companion Felix Jaeger are arguably the most infamous heroes of the Warhammer World. Follow their exploits in these novels from the Black Library.

Trollslayer

Trollslayer is the first part of the death saga of Gotrek Gurnisson, as retold by his travelling companion Felix Jaeger. Set in the darkly gothic world of Warhammer, Trollslayer is an episodic novel featuring some of the most extraordinary adventures of this deadly pair of heroes.

Skavenslayer

The second Gotrek and Felix adventure – Skavenslayer – is set in Nuln. The skaven are at large in the sewers beneath the city. The vile ratmen are determined to overthrow this bastion of humanity. Against such forces, what possible threat can just two hard-bitten adventurers pose?

Daemonslayer

Gotrek and Felix join an expedition northwards in search of the long-lost dwarf hall of Karag Dum. They set forth in an experimental dwarf airship. But greater and more sinister energies are coming into play, as a daemonic power is awoken to fulfil its ancient, deadly promise.

Dragonslayer

In the continuing saga of Gotrek and Felix, the duo find themselves pursued by the insidious skaven-lord, Grey Seer Thanquol. Dragonslayer sees the fearless duo back aboard a dwarf airship in a search for a golden hoard – and its deadly guardian.

Beastslayer

Storm clouds gather around the city of Praag as the hordes of Chaos lay siege to the lands of Kislev. Will Gotrek and Felix be able to prevent this ancient city from being overwhelmed by the massed forces of Chaos and their fearsome leader, Arek Daemonclaw?

Vampireslayer

As the forces of Chaos gather in the north to threaten the Old World, Gotrek and Felix are beset by a new, terrible foe. An evil from Sylvania threatens to reach out and tear the heart from our band of intrepid heroes.

Giantslayer

A darkness is gathering over the storm-wracked isle of Albion. With the aid of the mighty high elf mage Teclis, Gotrek and Felix are compelled to fight the evil of Chaos before it can grow to threaten the whole world.

ARE YOU READY TO TAKE COMMAND?

The WarCry CCG puts you in command of a huge army, prepared to drive your opponent to ruin on the battlefield. Are you ready to test your troop's mettle and your own strategic mind against that of your opponent? It all takes place in the Warhammer world with your favourite characters and races battling for dominance. Begin your career today by picking up a Starter Deck. Reinforce your army with new units ranging from powerful wizards to terrifying war machines by picking up booster packs from the latest expansions.
Your army is at your fingertips: are you ready to lead them?

BLAZE A TRAIL TO GLORY!

Gain access to elite units and participate in the ongoing storyline at

WWW.SABERTOOTHGAMES.COM

 Sabertooth Games | 610 Industry Dr | Tukwila, WA 98188

Warhammer, the Warhammer logo, and all imagery are trademarks of Games Workshop Ltd. WarCry and the WarCry logo are trademarks of Sabertooth Games.